HENRY AND BEEZUS

Enjoy All of Beverly Cleary's Books

BEEZUS AND RAMONA
DEAR MR. HENSHAW
ELLEN TEBBITS
EMILY'S RUNAWAY IMAGINATION
FIFTEEN
HENRY AND BEEZUS
HENRY AND RIBSY
HENRY AND THE CLUBHOUSE
HENRY AND THE PAPER ROUTE
HENRY HUGGINS
JEAN AND JOHNNY
THE LUCKIEST GIRL
MITCH AND AMY
THE MOUSE AND THE MOTORCYCLE
MUGGIE MAGGIE
OTIS SPOFFORD
RALPH S. MOUSE
RAMONA AND HER FATHER
RAMONA AND HER MOTHER
RAMONA FOREVER
RAMONA QUIMBY, AGE 8
RAMONA THE BRAVE
RAMONA THE PEST
RAMONA'S WORLD
RIBSY
RUNAWAY RALPH
SISTER OF THE BRIDE
SOCKS
STRIDER

And Don't Miss Beverly Cleary's Autobiography

A GIRL FROM YAMHILL
MY OWN TWO FEET

BEVERLY CLEARY

HENRY AND BEEZUS

Illustrated
by LOUIS DARLING

SCHOLASTIC INC.
New York Toronto London Auckland Sydney
Mexico City New Delhi Hong Kong Buenos Aires

ISBN 0-439-38594-6

Published by Scholastic Inc., 555 Broadway, New York, NY 10012,
by arrangement with HarperCollins Children's Books, a division of
HarperCollins Publishers.

24 23 22 21 20 19 18 17 16 15 5 6 7/0

Printed in the U.S.A. 40

First Scholastic printing, January 2002

Contents

HENRY AND BEEZUS

CHAPTER ONE

Ribsy and the Roast

HENRY HUGGINS stood by the front window of his square white house on Klickitat Street and wondered why Sunday afternoon seemed so much longer than any other part of the week. Mrs. Huggins was reading a magazine, and Mr. Huggins, puffing on his pipe, was reading the funnies in the Sunday *Journal*.

Henry's dog, Ribsy, was asleep in the middle of the living-room rug. As Henry looked at him, he suddenly sat up, scratched hard behind his left ear with his left hind foot, and flopped down again without even bothering to open his eyes.

Henry pressed his nose against the windowpane and looked out at Klickitat Street. The only person he saw was Scooter McCarthy, who was riding up and down the sidewalk on his bicycle.

"I sure wish I had a bike," remarked Henry to his mother and father, as he watched Scooter.

"I wish you did, too," agreed his mother, "but with prices and taxes going up all the time, I'm afraid we can't get you one this year."

"Maybe things will be better next year," said Mr. Huggins, dropping the funnies and picking up the sport section.

Henry sighed. He wanted a bicycle now. He could see himself riding up and down Klickitat Street on a shiny red bike. He would wear his genuine Daniel Boone coonskin cap with the snap-on tail, only he wouldn't wear the tail fastened to the hat. He would tie it to the handle bars so that it would wave in the breeze as he whizzed along.

"Henry," said Mrs. Huggins, interrupting his thoughts, "please don't rub your nose against my clean window."

"All right, Mom," said Henry. "I sure wish something would happen around here sometime."

"Why don't you go over to Robert's house? Maybe he can think of something to do," suggested Mrs. Huggins, as she turned a page of her magazine.

"O.K.," agreed Henry. Robert's mother said they couldn't give the white mice rides on Robert's electric train any more, but maybe they could think of something else. "Come on, Ribsy," said Henry.

Ribsy stood up and shook himself, scattering hair over the rug.

"That dog," sighed Mrs. Huggins.

Henry thought he had better leave quickly. As he and Ribsy started down the front steps, Robert came around the corner.

"What's up, Doc?" said Robert.

"Hi," responded Henry.

"My dad said maybe if I came over to your house, you could think of something to do," said Robert.

The boys sat down on the front steps. "Here comes old Scooter," observed Robert. The two boys watched the older boy pumping down the street on his bicycle. He was whistling, and not only was he riding without touching the handle bars, he even had his hands in his pockets.

"Hi," said Scooter casually, without stopping.

"Big show-off," muttered Robert. "I bet he takes that bike to bed with him."

"He sure thinks he's smart," agreed Henry. "He's been riding up and down all afternoon. Come on, let's go around in the back yard, where we won t have to watch old Scooter show off all day. Maybe we can find something to do back there."

Ribsy followed at the boys' heels. Unfortunately, the back yard was no more interesting than the front. The only sign of life was next door. A large yellow cat was dozing on the Grumbies' back steps, and there was smoke coming from the barbecue pit.

Robert looked thoughtful. "Does Ribsy ever chase cats?"

"Not that old Fluffy." Henry, understanding what was on Robert's mind, explained that Mrs. Grumbie sprinkled something called Doggie-B-Gone on her side of the rosebushes. Ribsy disliked the smell of it and was careful to stay on his side of the bushes.

Robert was disappointed. "I thought Ribsy might . . ."

"No such luck," interrupted Henry, looking at his dog, who had settled himself by the back steps to continue his nap. Henry picked a blade of grass and started to blow through it when the

WHATS
COOKIN
5 TABLESPOON
3 BAY
LEAVES
3 RIBS
CUP TOMATOES
½ LEMON

squeak-slam of the Grumbies' screen door made him look up. "Jeepers!" he whispered.

Stepping carefully over Fluffy, Mr. Hector Grumbie walked down the back steps. He was wearing a chef's tall white hat and an immense white apron. *What's cooking?* was written across the hat, and on the apron was printed a recipe for *Bar X Ranch Bar-B-Q Sauce.* Mr. Grumbie carried a tray full of bowls, jars, bottles, and what appeared to be bunches of dried weeds.

"Is he really going to cook?" whispered Robert.

"Search me," answered Henry. The two boys edged closer to the rosebushes that divided the two yards.

"Hello, Mr. Grumbie," said Henry.

"Hello there, Henry." Mr. Grumbie crossed the lawn and set the tray on the edge of the barbecue pit in the corner of his yard. He peeled a small object which he put into a bowl, sprinkled with salt, and mashed with a little wooden stick. Then he broke off pieces of the dried weeds and mashed them, too.

Henry and Robert exchanged puzzled looks.

"Need any help, Mr. Grumbie?" asked Henry.

"No, thank you." Mr. Grumbie poured a few drops of something into the mixture.

"Is that something that's supposed to be good to eat?" asked Robert. Mr. Grumbie didn't answer.

"What's that stuff in the bowl?" asked Henry.

"Herbs and garlic," answered Mr. Grumbie. "Now run along and play, boys. I'm busy."

Henry and Robert did not move.

"Etta!" called Mr. Grumbie to his wife. "I forgot the vinegar." He coughed as a breeze blew smoke in his face.

"I'll go get it for you," offered Henry, but his neighbor ignored him.

Squeak-slam went the screen. Mrs. Grumbie stepped over Fluffy and walked across the yard with a bottle in her hand. "Hector, can't we take your friends out to dinner instead of going to all this trouble?" she asked, as she fanned smoke out of her eyes.

"This is no trouble at all." Mr. Grumbie added a few drops of vinegar to the mixture in the bowl.

Henry thought Mrs. Grumbie looked cross, as she said, "Hector, why don't you let me cook the meat in the house? It would be so much easier and then we could bring it outside to eat."

"Now, Etta, I know what I'm doing." Mr. Grumbie poured a few drops from another bottle and mashed some more.

"But I don't like to see you spoil the flavor of a perfectly good piece of meat with all that seasoning. It would be different if you really knew how to cook." Mrs. Grumbie frowned, as she swatted at a bug circling over the sauce.

Mr. Grumbie frowned even more. "Anyone who can read a recipe can cook."

Mrs. Grumbie's face turned red, as she clapped

the bug between her hands, and said sharply, "Oh, is that so? What about the time you cut up tulip bulbs in the hamburgers because you thought they were onions?"

"That," said Mr. Grumbie, even more sharply, "was different."

Mrs. Grumbie angrily fanned smoke with her apron. "Just remember when we try to eat this mess you're fixing that it wasn't my idea. Even if the recipe is any good, the meat will probably be burned on the outside and raw inside. Smoke will get in our eyes and we'll be eaten alive by mosquitoes and . . ."

Mr. Grumbie interrupted. "Etta, we won't argue about it any more. I invited my friends to a barbecue and we're going to have a barbecue."

Henry and Robert were disappointed. They hoped the Grumbies would argue about it a lot more.

Then Mr. Grumbie looked at the recipe printed

on his apron. Because he was looking down at it, the words were upside down for him. "What does it say here?" he asked, pointing to his stomach.

Henry and Robert could not help snickering.

"Now, boys, run along and don't bother us. We're busy," said Mrs. Grumbie.

"Come on, Robert." Henry turned away from the rosebushes. He felt uncomfortable around Mrs. Grumbie, because he thought she didn't like him. At least, she didn't like Ribsy and that was the same as not liking Henry. He didn't want to make her any crosser than she was already, although secretly he couldn't see why she minded Ribsy's burying a bone in her pansy bed once in a while.

Henry tried standing on his hands just to show Mrs. Grumbie he wasn't paying any attention to what she was doing. Then he heard someone coming up his driveway. It was his friend Beezus and her little sister Ramona, who lived in the next

block on Klickitat Street. Beezus' real name was Beatrice, but Ramona called her Beezus, and so did everyone else. Beezus was carrying a baton and Ramona was riding a shiny new tricycle.

"Whoa!" yelled Ramona to her tricycle. Then she got off and tied it to a bush with a jumping rope.

"Hello," said Beezus. "See my baton."

The boys examined the metal rod, which was about two and a half feet long with a rubber knob at each end.

"What are you going to do with it?" asked Henry.

"Twirl it," said Beezus.

"I'll bet," scoffed Robert.

"I am too," said Beezus. "I take lessons every Saturday. By June I'll be good enough so I can twirl it in the Junior Rose Festival parade, and some day I'm going to be a drum majorette."

"June is only a couple of months away," said Henry, wondering what he would do in the parade this year. "Let's see you twirl it."

Beezus held the baton over her head and started to turn it with her right hand. It slipped from her fingers and hit her on the head.

"Boi-i-ing!" shouted the two boys together.

"You keep quiet," said Beezus crossly.

"Let me try," said Henry.

"No," answered Beezus, whose feelings were hurt.

"I didn't want to anyway." Henry started across the yard. "Come on, Robert, let's climb the cherry tree."

"All right for you, Henry Huggins!" shouted

Beezus, as the boys scrambled up through the branches. "I'm going home. Come on, Ramona, untie your horse."

But Ramona had seen Ribsy and she began to pat him on the head. Ribsy groaned in his sleep and sat up to scratch. Suddenly he was wide awake, sniffing the air.

"Wuf!" said Ribsy.

Henry could tell by the sound of the bark that Ribsy was excited about something. He peered out through the leaves of the cherry tree, but could see nothing unusual in his back yard. He saw Ribsy stand up, shake himself, and trot purposefully toward the Grumbies' back yard, with Ramona running after him.

Henry looked across the rosebushes and groaned at what he saw. On a platter beside the barbecue pit was a large piece of raw meat. The Grumbies were nowhere in sight.

"Here, Ribsy! Come here, boy!" called Henry

frantically, but Ribsy did not stop. "Catch him, Beezus!"

Ramona, who was trying to follow Ribsy through the rosebushes, shrieked.

"Hold still," directed Beezus, struggling with her little sister. "I can't get you loose from all these thorns when you wiggle that way."

"Come on, we better be getting out of here." Henry slipped and slid down the tree. "I bet the rain washed off the Doggie-B-Gone."

"I guess we better," agreed Robert cheerfully. After all, Ribsy wasn't his dog.

Henry hit the ground and tried to run through the rosebushes. Thorns clawed at his jeans and held him fast. "Here, Ribsy," he yelled. "Here, Ribs, old boy!"

Ribsy jumped for the roast.

With one desperate jerk, Henry tried to free himself from the roses. The thorns dug deeper into his legs.

Ribsy sank his teeth into the meat and pulled it to the ground.

Mr. Grumbie came through the back door with an armload of kindling. "Hey, stop that dog!" he yelled, dropping the wood on his toe. "Ow!" he groaned, as he started toward Ribsy and stepped on Fluffy's tail.

An ear-splitting yowl brought Mrs. Grumbie to the back porch. "Fluffy," she cooed, "did the man step on the precious pussycat's tail?"

Ribsy paused to take a firmer grip on the roast.

"If that cat hasn't any more sense than to sleep on the steps . . ." snapped Mr. Grumbie. "Hey, make that dog come back here!"

"Oh, my goodness!" exclaimed Mrs. Grumbie, when she saw what had happened. "Here, Ribsy, here, Ribsy!"

That was just what Ribsy needed to make him start running. He didn't like Mrs. Grumbie. He knew she sprinkled Doggie-B-Gone on the shrubbery to keep him away.

With one final yank and the sound of ripping cloth, Henry jerked away from the bushes.

"Tackle him," yelled Robert, who was still trying to untangle himself from the thorns.

Henry flung himself at his dog, but Ribsy raced on. Henry picked himself up off the Grumbies' driveway and ran after him.

Around the Grumbies' house he ran and on down Klickitat Street. He could hear Robert's and Mr. Grumbie's feet pounding down the sidewalk after him.

"Ribsy!" yelled Henry.

"Hey, come back here," shouted Robert.

"Stop thief!" bellowed Mr. Grumbie, holding onto his tall white hat with one hand.

Doors and windows began to open. "What's cooking, Grumbie?" someone called out.

Henry heard his mother say, "Oh, that dog!"

"Henry!" shouted Mr. Huggins.

"Go get 'em, Grumbie," yelled the man across the street.

Mr. Grumbie paused for breath. "Somebody head him off," he directed.

Ribsy ran into the street. A car turned the corner.

"Ribsy," wailed Henry, afraid to look.

"Hey, look out," warned Robert.

The car slammed on its brakes. Ribsy ran back to the sidewalk.

If only Henry could put on a burst of speed and make a really good flying tackle. But no matter how fast he ran, Ribsy was just out of his reach. He glanced over his shoulder and saw that Mr. Grumbie's face was red and he had lost his hat.

"Come . . . here . . . sir!" panted Mr. Grumbie. He wasn't used to running. Then his footsteps grew slower and slower until they stopped altogether.

Henry ran on, with Robert close behind. Their friend Mary Jane came out of her house and started down the sidewalk toward them. If only she would stop Ribsy.

"Catch him!" yelled Henry.

When Ribsy was only a few feet from Mary Jane, he dropped the meat on the sidewalk. Here was her chance. "Get it, Mary Jane," Henry shouted, with almost all the breath he had left. "Get the meat!"

Mary Jane stood staring at Ribsy.

"Pick up the meat, you dope!" yelled Robert.

Still Mary Jane did not move. Ribsy waited until Henry was almost within tackling distance before taking a firm grip on the roast and starting to run again.

"Mary Jane," panted Henry, "head him off."

Mary Jane stepped aside and Ribsy ran on. Henry felt as if he could not move another step.

"Why didn't you grab the meat?" he demanded, as he paused to catch his breath.

"You could have caught him if you wanted to," accused Robert.

"I couldn't either stop your dirty old dog," said Mary Jane. "Can't you see I'm wearing my Sunday School dress?"

"Mary Jane, you give me a pain." Henry glared at her.

"You're a poet and don't know it," said Mary Jane, twirling around to show off her full skirt.

Robert and Henry looked at one another. Girls!

Robert clutched Henry's arm and pointed in the direction from which Ribsy had come. "Look!"

A police dog, a fox terrier, and a sort of a collie were running down Klickitat Street toward Ribsy. Now there would be a dog fight, and the roast would be torn to pieces, and the two big dogs would chew up Ribsy. They would probably chew the fox terrier, too, and Henry knew the lady who owned him was very particular about keeping him out of dog fights. Henry would be blamed because the big dogs bit the little dog and . . . Suddenly Henry found he was too tired to do much of anything. He picked up a clod of dirt and threw it at the dogs as they passed him. "Beat it," he said, but he didn't bother to shout. He knew it was no use.

"Boy, a dog fight!" Robert was delighted. "This is going to be keen."

"Aw, keep quiet," said Henry. Robert wouldn't feel that way if Ribsy were his dog. The sort of collie was gaining on Ribsy, and the police dog was not far behind. Poor Ribsy! Henry shut his eyes. He couldn't stand seeing Ribsy chewed to pieces.

"Gangway everybody!" It was Scooter's voice. Leaning over his handle bars and pumping as hard as he could, he tore down the street behind the three dogs. He passed Henry and Robert and,

swerving to avoid the dogs, caught up with Ribsy. He didn't stop for the curb, but rode right over it with a tremendous bump. Then he flung himself off the bicycle and on top of Ribsy before the dog knew what was happening.

Ribsy dropped the meat and Scooter snatched it. He sprang on his bicycle, wheeled around in the middle of the street, and started back toward

the Grumbies' house, holding the meat above his head with one hand. The three other dogs and Ribsy all chased after Scooter, barking and growling as they jumped up and tried to snap at the meat.

Eluding them all, Scooter pedaled triumphantly back down Klickitat Street. "Hi," he said briefly to Henry and Robert, as he passed them.

"Hey, give me that meat," demanded Henry. Scooter ignored him.

"How do you like that!" said Robert. "He sure thinks he's smart."

Henry ran after Scooter, who pedaled even faster. Henry put on a burst of speed. So did Scooter. So did the dogs. Henry could hear the neighbors laughing. He tried to run faster, but Scooter stayed just out of his reach.

When Scooter reached the Grumbies' house, he handed the meat to its owner. "There you are, Mr. Grumbie," he said.

Mr. Grumbie took the battered roast. "Thank you, Scooter. That was mighty quick thinking on your part."

"It wasn't anything," said Scooter modestly. "It was easy to catch up with him on my bike."

The other dogs lost interest and ran away, but Ribsy continued to whimper and jump for the meat. Then even he gave up and sat panting, with his long pink tongue hanging out.

Poor Ribsy, thought Henry. He wanted that meat so much. Maybe he's tired of horse meat. Henry wished he dared to pet his dog, even though he had been cross with him.

"He's a dumb dog," said Scooter. "It's a good thing I came along and saved him from those other dogs when I did."

"I think you're mean, Scooter McCarthy," said Beezus. "Poor Ribsy."

"Why don't you go home?" said Henry to Scooter.

"Now, children," said Mrs. Huggins. Then she said to Mrs. Grumbie, "You must let us buy you another roast. Henry can help pay for it out of his allowance. He knows he is supposed to keep his dog out of your yard."

"Gee, my mother says roasts are expensive," said Scooter.

"You keep quiet." Henry scowled at Scooter. Why was Scooter always around when things happened to him? "Jeepers, I'm sorry, Mrs. Grumbie," said Henry. "I don't know what got into Ribsy. He was just hungry, I guess."

"He always is," observed Mr. Huggins.

Meat markets were closed on Sunday, but Henry knew that the delicatessen counter in the Supermarket was open. "Delicatessens have wienies, don't they?" he asked. "I could run down to the Supermarket and get some for you, if you'd like."

"I could go faster on my bike," said Scooter.

Mrs. Grumbie smiled. "Thank you, Henry. That won't be necessary. I think we'll go out to dinner." She looked at Mr. Grumbie, who had started toward the house with the roast. "Just between you and me," she whispered, "I don't think the meat would have been fit to eat with that sauce Mr. Grumbie was going to put on it." Then she called to her husband, "Hector, what are you going to do with that dirty piece of meat?"

"I suppose he might as well have it," said Mr. Grumbie reluctantly. "Not that he deserves it." He threw the remains to Ribsy.

Mrs. Grumbie paused in the doorway. "Henry, I'm going to bake cookies tomorrow. If you'll stop by on your way home from school tomorrow, I'll give you some."

"Thank you, Mrs. Grumbie," answered Henry. She seemed almost glad Ribsy had stolen the roast. At least, she wasn't cross any more.

"Here, Ribsy, it isn't time for you to eat yet." Henry tugged at the roast, but Ribsy hung on and growled. "Come on, Dad, give me a hand."

Mr. Huggins took hold of the meat and together they got it away from Ribsy. "I'll put it in the refrigerator for him," said Mr. Huggins, "and I'll have a talk with you later."

"Aw, gee, Dad," protested Henry. "I wasn't doing anything."

"You wanted something to happen, didn't you?" said Mr. Huggins, as he carried the meat into the house.

Henry did not answer. He just sighed and sat down on the steps. Why did these things always have to happen to him, anyway? Robert sat down beside him while Ramona sat on the grass beside Ribsy. Scooter picked up his bicycle. Beezus began to practice twirling her baton again.

"That was pretty exciting, wasn't it?" asked Robert. "It isn't often something happens around here on Sunday."

"I suppose so," said Henry, with no enthusiasm at all.

"It sure was a good thing I caught that dog of yours when I did," boasted Scooter.

Henry glared. "You think you're smart, don't you?"

"Well, somebody had to stop him." Scooter threw his leg across his bicycle.

"You just wait till I get my bike," said Henry.

Both boys looked interested. "Aw, you aren't going to get a bike," said Scooter. "You're just saying that."

"I am too going to get a bike," insisted Henry. "And it's going to be a better bike than yours. You just wait and see."

"When are you going to get it, Henry?" asked Robert.

"Never mind when." Henry tried to look mysterious. "You just wait and see."

"You're just saying that," repeated Scooter.

"He is not." Beezus flipped her baton and almost caught it before it fell to the grass. "If Henry says he's going to get a bicycle, he's going to get one. So there!"

"Ha," said Scooter, and pedaled down the street.

"Are you really going to get a bike?" asked

Robert and Beezus at the same time, when Scooter had gone.

"Sure, I'm going to get one." Henry tried to sound as if he meant it. He had to get a bike now. He just had to, that was all. He would start a bicycle fund right away. Of course, he had to think about paying for the roast first, but with all that beef in the refrigerator, he wouldn't have to buy horse meat for Ribsy at the Lucky Dog Pet Shop for a couple of weeks. The money he saved on horse meat would start his bike fund. He'd get that bicycle yet.

CHAPTER TWO

Henry Gets Rich

ONE day after school Mrs. Huggins asked Henry to run down to the market for a pound of ground round steak. On the way home he decided to cut through the vacant lot to see if he could find a coke bottle to turn in at the Supermarket for pennies to add to his bike fund. He was careful to keep the meat out of Ribsy's reach.

While Henry was looking for bottles, Ribsy, barking excitedly, bounded off into the bushes. Because it was so unusual for his dog to leave a package of meat, Henry followed to see what he was chasing. It was only a neighborhood cat, but when Henry started back to the path, he noticed a piece of gray cardboard with printing on it, sticking out of the bushes. He stopped to see what it was.

"Wow!" exclaimed Henry. Thrown carelessly in a hollow, and half hidden by weeds, was a pile of boxes. On the end of each box was printed the words *Double Bubble Gum.*

Telling himself the boxes were probably empty, Henry hastily hid the meat in a bush out of his dog's reach before he eagerly ripped open one of the boxes. It was full of pink balls the size of a marble. Henry popped one into his mouth, bit through the sugar coating, chewed vigorously, and then blew a rubbery pink bubble. It really was bubble gum!

Henry opened several other boxes and found them full of gum too. He couldn't take time to count the balls, but there must have been two hundred, maybe even three hundred, in each box. He counted the boxes. There were forty-nine, all

DOUBLE BUBBLE
DOUBLE BUBBLE GUM
DOUBLE BUBBLE GUM
DOUBLE BUBBLE GUM
DOUBLE BUBBLE GUM
DOUBLE BUBBLE GUM
DOUBLE BUBBLE GUM
DOUBLE BUBBLE GUM
DOUBLE BUBBLE GUM

full of bubble gum. Forty-nine times three hundred was . . . Well, it was a terribly big number.

Henry couldn't believe it. Forty-nine boxes of bubble gum, and three hundred balls in each box! It was enough to last the rest of his life. He would never have to park his gum again. He was rich!

Then Henry began to think. He knew he was rich only if he could get the gum home without being seen by the other boys and girls. That was not going to be easy. He took the pound of ground round steak out of the bushes and picked up two boxes of gum. "Come on, Ribsy," he said and ran home as fast as he could.

Henry tossed the package of meat onto the drain board in the kitchen and stowed the gum under his bed in his own room. Then he ran down Klickitat Street toward Beezus' house. He was careful to slow down when he saw her in the yard.

"Hi," said Henry, as if he had all the time in the world.

"Hello, Henry," said Beezus, gathering a handful of tulip petals and tossing them into the air so they fell over her in a pink shower. Her little sister Ramona was sitting on an apple box at the edge of the sidewalk.

"Say, Beezus," said Henry casually, "could I borrow your red wagon for a little while?"

"What for?" asked Beezus, looking much too interested.

"Oh, just an errand," said Henry.

"Can I go?" asked Beezus.

"No." Henry hid his impatience. "It's just some work I've got to do."

"Then you can't borrow it," said Beezus, and gathered another handful of petals.

Henry saw that this was a situation that must be handled carefully. "I'll give you a piece of bubble gum." He blew a bubble for her to admire.

"O.K.," agreed Beezus. "Give it to me and I'll get the wagon."

Henry knew she had him there. He hadn't put any loose gum in his pockets. He should have known better than to ask a favor of a girl, anyway. "I'll give it to you when I get back," he said.

Beezus was firm. "Not unless I go too."

Henry saw Scooter riding toward them on his bicycle and knew he had to act fast. He didn't want old Scooter hanging around asking questions. "O.K.," he agreed quickly. "You can go, but just remember I've got double dibs on what I'm going to bring home."

When Henry and Beezus returned from the back yard with the red wagon, Scooter was no longer in sight, but Ramona was still sitting on the apple box.

"Come on, Ramona," said Beezus, taking an old panda bear out of the wagon. "We're going with Henry."

"No," said Ramona.

Henry was growing anxious. What if Scooter

decided to cut through the vacant lot? "Jeepers, Beezus, we've just got to hurry. It's awfully important. If we don't get where we're going, we might be too late."

"Ramona," coaxed Beezus, "can't you play that game some other time?"

"What game?" asked Henry. He couldn't see that Ramona was playing any game.

"She's playing she's waiting for a bus," explained Beezus.

Henry groaned. It was the dumbest game he had ever heard of. "Doesn't she know it isn't any fun just to sit on a box?" he asked, looking nerv-

ously up and down the street. If only he could be sure no one else had discovered his gum!

"Sh-h," whispered Beezus. "She thinks it's fun and I don't want her to find out it isn't. It keeps her quiet." Then she said to her little sister, "If you get in the wagon, Henry and I'll pull you and you can pretend you're riding on the bus."

Henry was relieved that this idea pleased Ramona, who climbed into the wagon. He and Beezus ran down the street pulling the wagon behind them. When they came to the path through the vacant lot, Beezus pushed the wagon and Henry pulled. If only no one else had discovered Henry's treasure!

"Gee whillikers!" said Beezus in a hushed voice, when she saw what they had come for. "Are all those boxes really full of gum?"

"They sure are," said Henry, gathering an armload.

Beezus began to help. "And is it all yours?"

"Sure. I found it and said I had double dibs, didn't I?" said Henry. "But just to be sure, I've got to get it home before the other kids see it."

Beezus was a sensible girl who understood the importance of this, and she began to work faster. She lifted Ramona out of the wagon. Ramona yelled. "Here, chew this," said Beezus, poking a piece of gum into her mouth.

When Beezus and Henry had all the gum loaded onto the wagon, Henry took off his jacket and spread it over the boxes. Then they pulled their cargo home as fast as Ramona could run.

"Whew!" breathed Henry, when they turned into his yard. Now that the gum was on his property, no one could come along and say he had dibs on it too. He flung himself down on the front steps. "Come on," he said. "Let's chew."

Beezus helped herself to a ball of gum and crunched through the sugar coating. Henry added a ball to the one he already had in his mouth.

Ramona, too young to be an expert, smacked noisily. Henry gave Ribsy a piece. Looking puzzled, the dog tried to bite into it. The ball rolled around in his mouth until he spat it out on the grass and looked reproachfully at Henry.

Beezus admired the size of the bubbles Henry blew with a double wad, so she tried a second ball. Henry tried a third.

Then Robert came down the street. "What's up, Doc?" he asked.

"Look." Henry blew a bubble the size of a tennis ball. When it broke with a satisfying pop, he had difficulty getting the gum back into his mouth, because it stuck to his chin. "Have a piece. Have two pieces," he said, when he was able to talk.

"Wow!" Robert stared at the wagonload of gum. He lost no time in putting two pieces into his mouth.

The group chewed busily until Mary Jane appeared. "Henry Huggins, where did you get that gum?" she demanded.

"Have a piece." Henry ignored her question as he extended a box of gum to her.

"No, thank you," said Mary Jane. "My mother says chewing gum is vulgar." She watched the others chew until she could stand it no longer. "If you don't mind," she said, "I think I will try just one piece."

Henry pulled a bubble back into his mouth. "Sure, help yourself."

The first time Mary Jane tried to blow a bubble, she blew the gum out of her mouth onto the grass.

"No, that's not the way," said Henry, offering her another piece. "Flatten it with your teeth and poke your tongue into it before you blow."

After a little practice Mary Jane blew small, ladylike bubbles.

Then Scooter came pedaling down the street

on his bicycle. He stopped when he saw the group on the steps. "Say, Huggins, when are you going to get that bike?"

Henry blew an extra-large bubble before he answered. "You just wait and see."

Scooter whistled with amazement. "Say, where'd you get all that?"

"None of your beeswax," said Henry through his wad.

"How about letting me have a piece?" asked Scooter.

"Nope," said Henry.

"Aw, come on," coaxed Scooter.

"Nope." Henry was pleased that he had something Scooter wanted.

Scooter thought a minute. "I'll let you ride my bike to the corner and back if you'll give me a piece."

This put a new light on the matter. "Let me ride around the block," bargained Henry.

"O.K." Scooter got off his bicycle.

"Just one piece. Robert, you watch my gum while I'm gone." Henry picked up the bicycle. He wished he weren't so wobbly at riding, because he knew he would never hear the last of it if he took a spill in front of Scooter. He stepped on the high pedal with his left foot, threw his right leg across the seat, and found the other pedal with his right foot. The bike was too large for him, and he teetered from one side of the walk to the other before he got started.

Then Henry began to enjoy himself. This was the life! And if Scooter let him ride around the block for one piece of gum, there was no telling what he could get with the rest of the gum.

Henry started to make plans. He would use the gum the way the Indians used wampum. He would take some to school and see what the other boys and girls offered him. Why, they would probably even give him money for the gum. If he sold it for less than the store did, say two balls for a penny, he would get rid of it in no time and have the money for his bike fund. He'd show old Scooter yet!

The ride around the block was much too short. When he laid the bike on the lawn, Beezus said, "Henry, I need my wagon. I've got to take Ramona home. She's got gum in her hair."

"Sure," said Henry. "Here's a box of gum for letting me use the wagon."

"A whole box?" exclaimed Beezus gratefully. "Gee, thanks, Henry. I never expected this much."

As Beezus and her little sister left, Mr. Huggins pulled into the driveway and got out of his car. "Hello, kids," he said. "What's all this?"

When Henry explained, his father laughed and quickly estimated the total amount of gum. "Forty-nine boxes of three hundred balls each is . . . let's see . . . fourteen thousand seven hundred balls of gum. Quite a lot. isn't it?"

Even Scooter looked impressed until Mr. Huggins said, "How do you know there isn't something wrong with it?"

Four wads of gum were promptly spat into the shrubbery. Henry discovered his jaws were very tired. Come to think of it, there *was* something funny about all that gum lying around in a vacant lot.

"Or maybe it's stolen goods," suggested Mr. Huggins. "There must be some reason why it was dumped in the lot."

"Receiving stolen goods is pretty bad, isn't it?" asked Scooter.

"Aw, keep quiet," said Henry. "Gee, Dad, what do you think I better do?"

"Suppose I phone the police and ask them about it," suggested Mr. Huggins.

"O.K." Henry knew it was the right thing to do, but he didn't see how he could give up all that valuable gum. Not after his idea for building up his bike fund. And besides, it would really be something to show the kids at school.

After Mr. Huggins talked to the police, who said they would let him know what they found out about the gum, Henry spent an anxious evening. He stacked the boxes neatly under his bed, just in case he could keep them. Then he found he didn't feel much like reading or working on his model plane, so he wandered around the house, drumming his fingers on the windowpanes and waiting.

Finally Mrs. Huggins put down her knitting and said, "Henry, for heaven's sake, can't you light some place?"

Henry flung himself into a chair. "Gee, Mom, do you think they'll phone or drive up in a squad car?"

As if in answer to his question, the telephone rang. Henry held his breath while his father answered. "Yes," said Mr. Huggins. "Yes . . . yes

. . . I see. . . . It is? . . . Oh . . . yes. . . . Thank you for letting us know."

"What did they say, Dad? What did they say?" demanded Henry.

"The gum was thrown away by a man who owned a lot of gum machines and is going out of business," answered Mr. Huggins.

"I get to keep it then, don't I, Dad?"

Mr. Huggins smiled. "The police say there's no reason why you shouldn't keep it."

"I was afraid of that," sighed Mrs. Huggins. "Henry, how do you get mixed up in these things?"

"Boy, oh, boy!" Henry gloated. "Wait till I tell the kids at school!"

The next morning Mrs. Huggins didn't have to tell Henry to hurry. He and Ribsy left for school fifteen minutes early. On the way Henry chewed a couple of balls out of the box he was carrying, so he could show off some really good bubbles.

As soon as he reached Glenwood School, boys and girls began to crowd around him. "Did you get to keep all that gum Mary Jane said you found in the lot?" they asked.

"Sure I got to keep it," said Henry, disappointed at having his surprise spoiled. If that wasn't just like a girl, especially Mary Jane. "I'm going to sell it two for a penny."

The boys and girls knew a bargain when they saw one. "I'll take four," said Joey.

"Give me two," said Peter.

Some of the children did not have money with them, but Henry said they could bring it the next day. He opened charge accounts by writing their names and the amounts they owed on the margin of a comic book he had in the hip pocket of his jeans. By the time the second bell rang, Henry had twenty-two cents coming to him. Boy, oh, boy, he thought. This is even better than I expected.

By noon the news of Henry's treasure had spread throughout the school, and boys and girls from other rooms crowded around to buy the bargain gum. Henry was so busy selling that Beezus offered to write down the names of those who were going to bring their money the next day. By the time school was out, Henry had fifty-one cents in real money and forty-three cents written in his comic book. That was almost a dollar for his bike fund. Besides that, he had four marbles, a yo-yo, and six comic books.

And that was not all. Joey chose him to be the next blackboard monitor, Kathleen said she was going to invite him to her birthday party, six boys wanted to sit beside him in the cafeteria at noon, and Roger rode him home on his bicycle.

The next day Henry left even earlier and took another box of gum to school. He found business more complicated, because he not only had to sell gum and write down the names of the boys and girls who would bring their money the next day, he had to cross off in his comic book the names of those who had remembered to bring the pennies they owed him. He was glad when Beezus arrived and helped him keep the transactions straight.

At first, the boys and girls who were chewing Henry's gum were careful to chew only when Miss Bonner wasn't looking, but after a while they forgot to be careful. Then she said unexpectedly, "Henry, tell the class what mark of punctuation should go at the end of the sentence I have written on the blackboard."

Taken by surprise, Henry quickly shifted his

quid of gum to his cheek. "A period . . . uh . . . I mean a question mark," he said.

"I think, Henry," said Miss Bonner, "that if you throw your gum in the wastebasket, we shall all have much less trouble understanding you."

Feeling foolish, Henry walked to the front of the room and threw his wad of gum into the empty metal wastebasket. When it landed with a loud *clonk,* the whole class tittered.

"And now," said Miss Bonner, "I want everyone in the room who has gum in his or her mouth to throw it into the wastebasket."

Sheepishly, half a dozen boys and Beezus walked to the wastebasket and discarded their gum.

Miss Bonner looked around the room. "Robert," she said sternly. "George." The two boys slouched to the wastebasket.

After recess Miss Bonner marched another procession of gum chewers to the wastebasket. Although she didn't say much, Henry decided she looked pretty cross.

When Henry carried his gum out to the playground at noon, he found to his surprise that no one wanted to buy. Nearly everyone was already chewing and blowing.

"Maybe if you cut the price you could sell more," suggested Beezus.

"I guess I'll have to," said Henry. "I'll try four for a penny."

Business picked up after that, but when Henry went home after school, he wasn't sure how much money he had. He actually had thirty-one cents in his pocket, but when he tried to figure out the accounts in the comic book, he had to give up. Some of the boys who had forgotten to bring their money had charged more gum. Some had paid, but he had forgotten to cross off their names. Anyway, the comic book was getting so ragged and dirty, and the pencil marks so smudged, that it was impossible to read anything. Tossing the book into the fireplace, Henry decided he could remember how much Roger and Peter and a few more owed. He would just have to hope the others paid him.

The next morning when Henry was about to start to school with a box of gum, Beezus rang the doorbell. She handed Henry her box of bubble gum. "Mother says I have to give this back to you," she said.

"What for?" asked Henry.

"Because of Ramona. She gets into the gum and chews it and gets it stuck in her hair. The only

way Mother can get it out is to cut it out with the scissors. Ramona looks pretty awful with her hair all different lengths, and Daddy says if this keeps up she'll be bald before long." Beezus looked apologetic. "Anyway, I'm kind of tired of chewing gum."

When they reached the playground, Henry found business slow; everyone was already chewing gum. But when Henry cut the price to ten balls for a penny, he made several sales.

"Do you have any flavors beside cinnamon-peppermint or whatever it is?" asked Joey.

Henry had to admit he did not.

"Oh," said Joey, and went away.

Henry tried to think what stores did when they wanted to sell something. He knew they had sales, they advertised, and they gave away free samples. Henry had tried gum sales and he couldn't think of a good way to advertise, so he decided to try free samples. Although a dozen children crowded around him for samples, the demand was not as large as he had expected.

Then Roger, who owed Henry four cents for gum, approached him and asked for a free sample. Henry wasn't sure whether he should give gum to someone who owed him money, but since he had given it to the others, he gave Roger a piece. Roger put it in his pocket.

"How about that four cents you owe me for eight balls of gum you bought yesterday?" asked Henry.

"I forgot it," said Roger. "And anyway, how come you're giving gum away today when you sold it yesterday?"

"Well . . ." Henry didn't like to admit that no one was interested in his gum.

"Yes," said Peter, joining in the conversation. "I don't see why I have to pay you. You're giving it away now."

"I wasn't giving it away yesterday and the day before," said Henry. "I was selling it, so you owe me money."

"I do not." Peter blew a bubble that popped.

"You do too," said Henry, feeling confused.

The bell rang, and they started toward their classroom. Henry noticed Peter and Roger talking to each other. Then they gathered a bunch of children around them outside the door. They talked earnestly together until Miss Bonner herded them into the room.

Now what are they up to? thought Henry. He worried about it all through social studies and arithmetic. Somehow, things didn't seem to be turning out the way he had planned. He was secretly pleased when Miss Bonner made Peter throw his gum in the wastebasket.

When recess came, Henry was surprised at the number of boys and girls who suddenly wanted free gum. He had almost as big a crowd around him as he had had on the first morning. He began to enjoy himself again.

Then Roger and Peter called to him. "Hey, Henry, can we see you a sec?"

"Sure," said Henry, stepping away from the others.

"Here's the gum I owe you." Roger handed Henry eight balls of bubble gum.

"Mine, too." Peter held out four balls.

"Hey, now wait a minute," protested Henry. "That's not fair."

"It is too," said Roger. "We bought gum from you and now we're returning it instead of paying for it."

"But you chewed it," objected Henry. "I saw you, and Miss Bonner made you throw it in the wastebasket."

"This gum hasn't been chewed, has it?" asked Peter.

Henry had to admit it hadn't.

"Then why can't we return it, like in a department store?" demanded Roger.

Baffled, Henry took the gum. Something was wrong some place, but he couldn't figure out what. He did know one thing, that was sure There went six cents out of his bike fund.

Then Mary Jane ran up to Roger and Peter. "Did he take the free samples we collected for you?" she asked.

"Well, how do you like that!" exclaimed Henry. "That's cheating, that's what it is."

"It is not," said Mary Jane. "You gave us the gum and if we want to give it to someone else, that's our business."

Henry looked glum. He supposed it was her business. Mary Jane was one of those annoying girls who were always right. The worst of it was, now he couldn't expect the others to pay. Henry was actually glad when the bell ended recess, even though he knew spelling came next.

That day no one chose Henry to be a monitor, and only Robert sat with him in the cafeteria. He heard Kathleen say she thought she wouldn't invite any boys to her birthday party.

After lunch, when the class was settled with its readers, the room door opened and Miss Mullen, the principal, entered. She whispered to Miss Bonner and then turned to the class. "Boys and girls," she announced, "I want to talk to you for a few minutes this afternoon. We have a problem at Glenwood School that we all should discuss."

Now what? thought Henry. Probably running in the halls again or writing on the building with chalk.

Miss Mullen looked around the room. Then she said, "That problem is gum."

Henry felt his neck and ears grow hot. He was sure everyone in the room was looking at him.

Miss Mullen continued. "There has been more gum chewing than usual at Glenwood School in the last few days. I wonder if someone can tell me why it is not a good idea to chew gum in school."

The class was silent.

"Can't someone give me a reason?" she asked. "Henry Huggins, why do you think it is not a good idea to chew gum in school?"

Henry's ears felt as if they were on fire. He hadn't known Miss Mullen even knew his name. "Uh . . ." he said. Why couldn't he think of something to say? "Well . . ." He had to think of something. "It . . . uh . . . well . . . uh . . . I guess it is . . . lots of trouble for teachers to make kids throw it in the wastebasket." The words came out in a rush. At least, he had said something.

"That is an excellent reason," said Miss Mullen. "Chewing gum wastes valuable time. Who else can give me a reason?"

One of the girls timidly raised her hand and

said, "Sometimes it gets stuck on the floor and things."

"Splendid," said Miss Mullen. "I was hoping someone would mention that, because our janitor tells me he has spent most of his time in the last few days scraping gum off the floors and desks."

The class began to feel less shy and was suddenly full of reasons why gum should not be chewed in school.

Then Mary Jane raised her hand and said, "Miss Mullen, I know where the gum is coming from."

Leave it to old tattletale Mary Jane, thought Henry. And after I showed her how to blow bubbles, too.

Miss Mullen said, "That isn't important, Mary Jane. What is most important is that so many boys and girls have been chewing gum in school."

What a relief! At least, Miss Mullen wasn't going to point him out in front of everyone.

Miss Mullen smiled at the class. "Now that we have talked about our problem, I wonder how many boys and girls have decided not to chew gum in school any more."

Thirty-five hands shot into the air. "Splendid," exclaimed the principal. "I knew I could count on Miss Bonner's room to co-operate."

When Miss Mullen left, Roger whispered across the aisle to Henry, "Now see what you've done."

"Aw, keep quiet," answered Henry out of the corner of his mouth, as he bent over his reader. He knew one thing. Even though the class forgot its promise in a few days, he wouldn't be able to sell any gum around Glenwood for a long time.

After school he wasted no time in finding Mary Jane. "Tattletale!" he yelled.

"Pooh to you," answered Mary Jane, with her nose in the air. "Everybody's tired of your old gum anyway. It's all that funny cinnamon-peppermint flavor."

"Come on, Ribsy," said Henry to his dog, who had been waiting under the fir tree. He popped a ball of gum into his mouth, chewed, and blew a halfhearted bubble that broke with a little *spip.* He spat out the gum. Somehow, he didn't enjoy cinnamon-peppermint flavor any more.

When Henry reached home, he threw his jacket and Daniel Boone cap onto a chair and went straight to the refrigerator. "Hi, Mom!" he said to Mrs. Huggins, who was frosting a chocolate cake. "That sure looks good."

"You may lick the bowl when I'm finished." Mrs. Huggins swirled the icing in a pattern on the cake. "And by the way, I want to talk to you."

With a swipe of his finger, Henry wiped a drop of frosting from the edge of the bowl. It was peppermint-flavored.

"Henry, your hands aren't very clean," said his mother. "It's about those boxes of gum you have under your bed. How do you expect me to run the vacuum cleaner in your room? Why don't you give the gum to your friends? I'm sure they'd be glad to have it."

Henry sighed. That was all his mother knew about his friends. Suddenly he found it made his jaws tired just to think about all those boxes and boxes of gum. He didn't want to think about it. Gum—ugh!

"O.K., Mom," he agreed. "I'll get rid of it. And don't bother saving the bowl for me to lick."

Henry and Ribsy went out onto the front porch. As Henry was wondering how he would get rid of the gum, Scooter rode by and called out, "Miss Mullen was sure on the warpath because of your old gum. She went to every room in the school. I bet you caught it."

"I did not," said Henry. "And anyway, what do I care?" That's right, he thought, what do I care?

He had saved over a dollar for his bike fund, even if he couldn't expect to collect from the rest of the people who owed him money. Not only had he earned some bike money, he had been famous for a few days, too. And for once in his life he had chewed all the gum he wanted. So had his friends. More than they wanted.

It did not take Henry long to make up his mind. "Come on, Ribsy," he said, and ran down the street to Beezus' house.

When Beezus and her little sister came to the door, Henry stared at Ramona. "Jeepers!" he exclaimed. "What happened to her?" Almost all the hair was cut off the left side of her head. The right side was jagged.

"Doesn't she look awful?" asked Beezus. "After

Mother cut the gum out of her hair, she got hold of the scissors and cut it herself. She says she wants to be bald like our Uncle Jack."

Henry groaned. Now probably everyone would say this was his fault. It certainly was funny the way he kept getting into trouble just because of a bunch of old gum. He would be glad when he saw the last of it. "Say, Beezus," he said, "could I borrow your red wagon again? I'm going to take that gum back to the lot and dump it where I found it."

"Sure, you can borrow it," answered Beezus. "Come on. I'll help."

CHAPTER THREE

The Untraining of Ribsy

ONE Saturday afternoon Henry was sitting on the front steps amusing Ribsy by throwing a stick for him to retrieve. Every time Henry tossed the stick out onto the lawn, Ribsy bounded after it, brought it back, and dropped it at Henry's feet. Then Ribsy wagged his tail and waited for Henry to throw the stick again. Henry decided that since his dog was so smart about fetching sticks, he would teach him to bring his father's slippers or something useful.

While Henry and Ribsy were playing, Scooter McCarthy rode up on his bicycle and tossed the

Huggins' copy of the *Journal* onto the grass. "Say, Huggins," he said, "I'm going to Scout Camp during Easter vacation next week and I wondered if you knew anybody I could get to take my paper route while I'm gone."

Henry tossed the stick for Ribsy again. "I'll take it, Scooter. I've always wanted to deliver papers."

Scooter looked doubtful. "Aw, you're not old enough."

Henry knew that *Journal* carriers had to be eleven years old, but he said, "It wouldn't matter for three days, would it? It would still be your route and I'd just be a substitute. Aw, come on, Scoot. Let me do it."

"You don't have a bike," said Scooter, "and I could only pay a dollar."

"I could walk," said Henry. "And it's all right about the dollar, too." He wouldn't admit it to Scooter, but he thought a dollar would be a lot of money to add to his bike fund all at once. "Please,

Scooter. I won't make any mistakes or anything."

"I've got some pretty cross customers on my route," warned Scooter. "That old Mrs. Jones phones the *Journal* office if just one teeny corner of her paper gets in the mud, and Mrs. Green gets mad if I throw the paper in her flower boxes. You've got to be careful when you deliver papers."

"I could do it," said Henry. "I'd be real careful. Honest, I would."

"We-l-ll." Scooter thought a minute. "All right. You can take the route, but you better not get me in trouble. I'll give you a list of customers next week."

"Gee, thanks, Scooter," said Henry gratefully.

Jeepers, another dollar for his bike fund! Henry made up his mind he'd do such a good job delivering papers that Scooter would want him to take the route when he went away during summer vacation. Then he would really make some money for the fund. He could see himself walking down

Klickitat Street throwing papers onto porches with an experienced flip of his wrist. Still better, he pictured himself riding down the street on a shiny red bike with his snap-on raccoon tail floating from the handle bars. Boy, oh boy, he was getting closer to that bike all the time.

Then he noticed the tightly rolled *Journal* lying on the lawn. That gave him an idea. Instead of training Ribsy to fetch his father's slippers, he would teach him to bring in the paper every night. "Fetch, Ribsy," he said. "Fetch the paper."

Ribsy sat thumping his tail on the lawn.

"Aw, come on." Henry picked up the paper and held it under Ribsy's nose. Then he threw it. Still Ribsy sat. He was used to fetching sticks, not newspapers. He turned and chewed at a flea on his back.

"Come on, you old dog." Henry showed Ribsy the paper again. Ribsy glanced at it and settled himself with his nose on his paws. Henry threw the paper half a dozen times, but Ribsy paid no attention. Thinking how silly he must look, throwing a paper and fetching it himself while his dog watched, Henry held the *Journal* behind his back. With his other hand he picked up the stick. "Ribsy, look," he ordered.

At the sight of the stick Ribsy sprang to his feet. "Wuf," he said, wagging his tail expectantly.

Henry pretended he was going to throw the stick. Instead, he tossed the paper. Before he knew the difference, Ribsy bounded after it and caught it in his mouth.

When the dog dropped the paper at his feet, Henry patted him. "Good dog, Ribsy," he said. "Good old Ribsy."

Ribsy wriggled, and wagged his tail with delight. The next time Henry threw the paper, he sprang to fetch it. "Good dog," Henry said approvingly. "I guess you're just about the smartest dog around here."

The next day was Sunday. Henry, who always woke up earlier than his mother and father, decided to read the funnies in the *Journal,* which was delivered early on Sunday morning. He tiptoed out to the porch, expecting to pick up the paper as he always did. Instead, he stood staring in horror at what he saw. There was not just one *Journal* on the door mat. There was a whole pile of them. Ribsy sat beside the papers, wagging his tail and looking pleased with himself.

Henry groaned. "Did you pick up all these and

bring them here?" he asked Ribsy in a whisper.

Thump, thump, thump. Ribsy wagged his tail. Then he stood up and wagged his whole body.

"You old dog," muttered Henry crossly, as he counted the papers. There were seventeen *Journals* on his door mat. Fortunately, the *Oregonian* carrier was late this morning. What if Ribsy had collected two kinds of newspapers and piled them on the door mat?

Seventeen *Journals!* Henry wondered how he could ever face Scooter. And now he wouldn't get to earn the dollar. He wouldn't get to deliver papers when Scooter went to camp during summer vacation. But worst of all was the way Scooter would behave after this. He would never, never forget that Henry's dog had got him in trouble with his *Journal* customers.

Henry scowled at Ribsy, who looked puzzled because he hadn't been praised for retrieving all those papers. Henry knew he had to think of something, and fast, too. Then he remembered that Klickitat Street was the beginning of Scooter's route, and because it was so early, Scooter was probably still delivering papers.

"Come on, Ribsy," he ordered, hurrying into his room. There he pulled on jeans and a sweater over his pajamas and shoved his feet into sneakers. He shut Ribsy in the room, grabbed the papers on the porch, except for one copy which he tossed into the living room, and ran down the street as fast as he could to Scooter's house.

No one on Klickitat Street was up at that hour, and Henry was relieved to see the blinds still down on Scooter's house. He tiptoed up the front steps and, after looking uneasily up and down the street and listening for sounds from within the house, laid the sixteen *Journals* on the door mat. Then he ran home as fast as he could.

After entering as quietly as he could, Henry threw himself on his bed with a gasp of relief. No one had seen him! Scooter would never know how the sixteen papers found their way back to his door mat. The dollar for the bike fund was safe.

Henry felt unusually cheerful after his narrow escape and was enjoying a second helping of hot cakes when the doorbell rang. Mr. Huggins answered it, and Henry heard Scooter say, "Here's your paper, Mr. Huggins. I'm sorry it was late."

Holding his breath, Henry looked at the breakfast table, strewn with the Sunday *Journal.*

Mr. Huggins said, "There must be some mistake, Scooter. We have our paper."

"You have?" Scooter sounded surprised. "You're the only people on Klickitat Street that have one."

"Henry, where did you find the paper this morning?" asked Mr. Huggins.

"On the door mat." Well, he *had* found it on the door mat. His father didn't ask what else he had found, did he?

"It sure is funny," repeated Scooter. "I know I

delivered all the papers, but . . . well, thanks anyway, Mr. Huggins. It sure is funny."

Jeepers, thought Henry. Now he had done it. Why hadn't he thought of putting his own paper on Scooter's door mat along with the others? Now Scooter would get suspicious and might figure out what had happened.

Mr. Huggins folded back the sport section. "Isn't it funny that Scooter's papers should disappear from Klickitat Street?" he remarked to no one in particular. "When I used to deliver papers when I was a kid, I had a lot of trouble with dogs stealing them."

Henry looked sharply at his father, but Mr. Huggins appeared to be interested in the paper. "What did you do about it?" asked Henry, as if he were just making polite conversation.

"Sprinkled red pepper on the papers for a while until the dogs learned to leave them alone," answered Mr. Huggins, pouring himself another cup of coffee.

After breakfast Henry waited until his mother had finished the dishes. Then he quietly found the can of red pepper and an old newspaper and called Ribsy out into the back yard, where he was sure Scooter couldn't see him.

He rolled the paper, sprinkled it with red pepper, and threw it out on the grass. Ribsy ran over to it, stopped, and sniffed. He walked all the way around the paper, sniffing. Then he rolled it over with his paw before he picked it up carefully by one end and dropped it at Henry's feet. He wagged his tail and looked pleased with himself.

"You old dog," said Henry crossly.

Ribsy jumped up on Henry and looked so eager that Henry couldn't help petting him. "What am I going to do with you, anyway?" he asked. Then he sprinkled pepper on the paper again and tossed it onto the grass. Ribsy bounded after it. Again he sniffed, and rolled the paper with his paw before he picked it up and carried it to Henry.

Henry had a feeling that although pepper might work with other dogs, it wasn't going to work with Ribsy. Anyway, he couldn't follow two paper boys around and sprinkle pepper on every single paper they delivered, could he? And then there was the *Shopping News* besides. He would spend all his bike fund buying pepper.

Henry sat down to think of another way to untrain Ribsy. He couldn't keep the dog shut in the house alone very long, because he would howl and scratch on the door to get out. Mrs. Huggins didn't like scratches on her woodwork, and the neighbors didn't like to hear Ribsy howl. He couldn't tie the dog up, either. It never took Ribsy long to chew through a rope or leash.

Henry tried to think what Ribsy didn't like. He didn't like to have his tail pulled. Henry thought about pulling his tail every time he picked up a paper, but that would hurt Ribsy. Ribsy didn't like the egg he was supposed to eat once a week so he would have a glossy coat, but Henry didn't see how he could give him an egg every time he stole a paper. Henry couldn't think of anything else Ribsy didn't like except baths. Ribsy was really a very agreeable dog.

While Henry was still trying to think of a way to untrain Ribsy, he heard Scooter calling. He quickly put the pepper and the paper inside the back door and ran around the house. What would he say if Scooter guessed?

"Hi! Sure is funny how you got a paper when nobody else on this street did, isn't it?"

"Yeah," said Henry, wondering how he could change the subject.

"And you know what?" asked Scooter.

"What?" said Henry, knowing very well what.

"I know I delivered those papers, and when I

got home I found sixteen papers on my porch."

"Jeepers!" Henry did his best to look surprised. Why couldn't a fire engine or something come down Klickitat Street right now? He heard the jingle of Ribsy's license tag. The dog trotted around the corner of the house and, after scratching, settled himself at Henry's feet. Then he suddenly sat up and looked toward the Grumbies' house next door.

Henry looked too, and what he saw gave him a terrible sinking feeling in his stomach. There in plain sight on the front steps lay the Grumbies' *Oregonian.*

Ribsy jumped to his feet, and Henry knew he had to do something in a hurry or Ribsy would retrieve the Grumbies' paper before Scooter's very eyes. Shuddering at the thought of what would happen if he did, Henry hastily grabbed his dog around the neck.

"Good old Ribsy," he said, hanging on tight.

Ribsy squirmed. Henry wished as hard as he could that Scooter would go home.

"If anything happens to the papers tomorrow afternoon, I guess I better not go to Scout Camp," said Scooter. "If I lose my route, I won't have the money to go to camp during summer vacation."

Henry didn't answer. He was too busy trying to hang onto Ribsy without looking as if he were holding him. Ribsy strained toward the Grumbies' paper. Henry turned the dog's head in the opposite direction, but the minute he let go, Ribsy whimpered and tried to get at the paper.

"What's the matter with that dog, anyway?" asked Scooter. "Why don't you let him go?"

"He doesn't want to go," said Henry. "Do you, Ribsy?"

Ribsy whimpered and struggled to get out of Henry's arms. Henry couldn't see why Scooter had to hang around so long, anyway. Why couldn't he go home?

Henry tried not to look at the paper on the Grumbies' front steps, but it was all he could think about. Then the Grumbies' front door opened, and Mr. Grumbie, wearing his bathrobe and slippers, walked sleepily out on the porch, picked up the paper, and went into the house again.

Ribsy relaxed and Henry let go of him. Whew! That was close. Henry looked anxiously up and down the street to see if he could see any other papers. Instead he saw Beezus and her little sister Ramona.

The two girls stopped in front of Henry's house. Beezus had a handful of waxed paper. Ramona had a red plastic water pistol. She looked at Scooter, aimed, and shot a stream of water into his face. "You're dead," she announced.

"I am not, and you cut that out." Scooter wiped his face with his sleeve.

"Ramona, stop that or I'll have to take the pistol away from you," ordered Beezus. "Henry, come on over to the park with us. I've got a bunch of bread wrappers to sit on when we slide on the slides."

"O.K.," said Henry promptly, more because he wanted to get away from Scooter than because he wanted to go to the park. Still, it was a long time since he had waxed the slides by sitting on a bread wrapper. "Here, Ribsy," he called.

Ribsy bounded out of the shrubbery with his license tag jingling. In his mouth was a *Shopping News,* yellow with age, which he dropped at Henry's feet. Henry didn't have the courage to look at Scooter. Ribsy bounded into the bushes and came out with another old paper. Then he stood wagging his tail and looking at Henry.

"I thought so, Henry Huggins," said Scooter accusingly. "I thought you knew something about my papers disappearing."

"Well, maybe . . ." Henry didn't know what to say. Now he really was in trouble. A stream of

water from Ramona's pistol hit him in the eyes. "Aw, cut it out," he said, wiping his face. As if he didn't have enough trouble without a little kid shooting him with a water pistol!

"I bet you trained that mutt of yours to steal papers." Scooter was really angry. "I suppose you're going to let him steal my papers all the time and make me lose my route."

"No, he won't," promised Henry. "I'll untrain him . . ."

"You better untrain him," interrupted Scooter angrily. "And I'm going to find somebody else to take my route while I'm gone, too. I have enough trouble with papers getting in the mud and stuff, without having your old mutt going around stealing them."

"You got the papers delivered again this morning before anybody complained, didn't you?" asked Henry.

"Yes, because I started extra early in the first place, that's why. But what about tomorrow, when I have to deliver them after school?"

That was just what Henry had been asking himself. What about tomorrow? He had to think of something fast if he didn't want to lose a dollar from his bike fund. "I'll tell you what, Scooter. You make me a list of your customers and I'll deliver the papers tomorrow night free of charge. And if I do it right and Ribsy doesn't take any, I get to deliver the papers while you're gone. How about it?" Henry waited anxiously for Scooter's answer.

"That's fair," said Beezus.

Scooter scowled and thought over Henry's offer. "O.K.," he said at last. "Maybe that way you'll be sure to untrain him."

"It's a deal," said Henry. Now all he had to do was figure out how to keep Ribsy from stealing papers.

Scooter started home and then turned back. "But just you remember, if you make me lose my route, I'll, I'll . . . Well, I'll do something."

While the two boys were arguing, Robert had joined the group in the front yard. "Scooter is pretty mad, isn't he?" he asked. "I'm glad I'm not in your shoes."

"Yeah." Henry looked at the papers at his feet. "Jeepers, how am I going to get Ribsy untrained by tomorrow afternoon? Nothing I try works."

"It's easy," said Robert. "You've got to make him afraid of what he steals. Hit him with a paper a few times and he'll get the idea."

"I'll try," said Henry, "but I bet it won't work with Ribsy."

"Don't hit him too hard," begged Beezus.

Ribsy came trotting across the lawn with an old paper in his mouth. When he dropped it at Henry's feet, Henry picked it up and rapped him on the head with it. He didn't hit hard enough to hurt, but just hard enough so he would get the idea. Ribsy was delighted. He growled a pretended growl and grabbed the paper. Henry hung on and so did Ribsy. Wagging his tail, the dog growled and tugged. Henry managed to yank the paper away.

This time he hit Ribsy harder. Ribsy gave a joyful bark and sprang at the paper. He snatched it from Henry and worried it. Then he settled down to chew it to pieces.

"See what I mean?" said Henry. It was bad enough to have a dog that stole papers, but it was worse to have one that chewed them to bits. Henry could see Klickitat Street strewn with chewed-up *Journals* and he tried to picture what Scooter would do. Whatever it was, he didn't like to think about it.

After school the next day Henry joined Ribsy, who was waiting under the fir tree, and ran home with his dog as fast as he could. Then he changed into his after-school clothes, fixed himself some bread and peanut butter, and, after shutting Ribsy in his room, went out on the front porch to wait for Scooter.

In a few minutes Robert joined him. "Thought of anything yet?" he asked.

"No," admitted Henry. "I shut Ribsy in the house, but he won't stay there long."

Ribsy appeared at the window with his front feet on the sill. He whimpered and scratched at the glass with one paw.

"Go away," ordered Henry.

Ribsy ran to the front door, where Henry could

hear him scratching on the wood. Then Mrs. Huggins opened the door and said, "Henry, you'll just have to keep this dog outdoors with you."

"O.K., Mom," answered Henry, looking at Robert. "See what I mean?"

Then Beezus and her little sister Ramona joined

the boys on the steps. Ramona promptly shot Robert with her water pistol. "You're dead!" she shouted.

Robert wiped his face with his sleeve. "I am not dead. I can't be dead if I'm not playing, can I?"

Then Scooter appeared, lugging a bundle of newspapers which he threw down on the walk in front of Henry's house. He handed Henry a list of addresses. "Be sure you remember about Mrs. Green's flower boxes," he said. "And I better not get any complaints about missing papers tonight or any other night."

"You won't," said Henry, but he didn't sound very sure about it.

Ramona fired a shot at the departing Scooter. Beezus said, "Come on, we'll help you."

Keeping a wary eye on Ramona's water pistol, the other three began to roll newspapers. Henry was so busy watching the pistol that he forgot to watch Ribsy. Before he knew it, the dog had snatched a paper and had begun to worry it to pieces.

"Ribsy!" yelled Henry. "Drop that!"

Ribsy shook the paper harder. Henry grabbed one end of the paper. Ribsy hung on.

Then Ramona raised her water pistol and aimed. A stream of water hit Ribsy in the face. "You're dead!" shouted Ramona, and Ribsy dropped the paper. Looking puzzled, he backed away and shook himself.

"Hey! Did you see that?" Henry jumped up and tripped over the papers in his excitement. "Ribsy dropped the paper! Ramona made him drop the paper. Do it again, Ramona."

"No," said Ramona.

"Aw, come on," coaxed Henry. "Beezus, make her shoot Ribsy again. This has just got to work."

"No," said Ramona.

Scooter came riding down the street on his bicycle. "You started delivering my papers yet?" he asked.

"In a minute," said Henry. "You just wait. Everything's going to be all right."

"It better be." Scooter looked threatening as he

rode away. "And you better get going," he yelled back.

Henry ran into the house and found his own plastic water pistol. After loading it at the kitchen sink, he ran outdoors and threw a paper at Ribsy. When the dog picked it up, Henry let him have a stream of water right in the face. Ribsy dropped the paper and backed away. Looking puzzled and embarrassed, he shook himself.

"It works!" shouted Henry. "It really works! I'm going to get Ribsy untrained after all." He ran into the house again and filled his army-surplus canteen with water, in case he needed to reload his pistol.

Beezus and Robert had the papers rolled and stuffed into the canvas bag, which Henry now lifted over his head. The *Journals* were heavier than he expected. "Come on," he said. "Let's go."

By then Beezus had succeeded in getting the

water pistol away from Ramona. "I'll help you keep Ribsy covered," she said.

Henry threw a *Journal* onto the lawn of the first house on the list. Ribsy bounded after the paper, but the minute he opened his mouth to pick it up, Henry and Beezus shot him with two streams of water. Looking surprised and unhappy, Ribsy backed away from the paper and shook himself.

The next time Henry threw a paper, Ribsy approached it cautiously. The instant he touched it, Beezus and Henry opened fire. This time Beezus shot from the hip.

"You're dead!" shrieked Ramona. Ribsy decided he wasn't interested in the paper after all.

The third time Henry threw a paper, Ribsy ignored it. He was too busy sniffing a bush even to look at it.

"Good dog," said Henry, bending over to pet him. The weight of the papers in the canvas bag nearly tipped him over.

Ribsy wagged his tail. "Good old Ribsy," said Henry proudly. Ribsy was untrained at last.

When the children returned after delivering all the papers without a single mistake, they found Scooter waiting on the front steps. "How many did your mutt run off with?" he wanted to know.

"He isn't a mutt and he didn't run off with any,"

boasted Henry. "He wouldn't touch a paper. See?" Henry tossed his own copy of the *Journal* onto the grass. Ribsy looked the other way.

"I guess I did a pretty good job of delivering papers," bragged Henry. "You won't get any complaints tonight."

"That's right," agreed Beezus. "I checked every address on the list with him just to make sure."

Scooter threw one leg over his bicycle.

"And I get to deliver papers while you're away, don't I?" Henry was thinking of his bike fund again, now that Ribsy was untrained.

"Sure," said Scooter, "if you don't think it's too hard work for a kid without a bike."

"You just wait," said Henry. "I bet I get that bike sooner than you think."

"Ha," said Scooter, pedaling down the street.

"You're dead!" shrieked Ramona, squirting her pistol with deadly accuracy.

CHAPTER FOUR

Henry Parks His Dog

ONE Friday after school Henry was fixing himself a snack of bread, peanut butter, and strawberry jam when the doorbell rang.

"Come in, Beezus," he heard his mother say.

As Henry went into the living room, he held up his bread and licked the jam that had run down his wrist. Beezus and her little sister Ramona each held a gnawed cabbage core. They had stopped eating because they were too polite to eat in front of people.

Beezus handed Henry a newspaper clipping. "I thought maybe you'd like to see this."

"Bikes for Tykes," was the headline. "Lost Bicycles up for Sale Tomorrow."

"Hey, maybe you've got something." Henry read faster.

"Enough bicycles—some hundred or more—have been found by the police this past year to equip half a company of soldiers, and tomorrow at ten A.M. they go up for auction at the Glenwood police station."

This was Henry's chance. "Hey, Mom, look! Isn't an auction where somebody holds up something and everybody says how much he'll pay for it and the one who says the most gets it?"

"Yes, it is," answered Mrs. Huggins, as she read the clipping.

"Boy! I've got four dollars and fourteen cents saved. I bet I can get a bike for that much." Henry pictured a hundred soldiers riding by on bicycles —and one of those bicycles was meant for him. He'd show old Scooter yet.

Mrs. Huggins looked doubtful. "I wouldn't be too sure," she advised. "After all, there must be some reason why the bicycles haven't been claimed. If you lost a bicycle you'd try to get it back, wouldn't you?"

"Yes," agreed Henry, who was sure most of the bicycles belonged to rich boys who had so many bikes they didn't miss one when they lost it. "But I can go, can't I, Mom?"

"Yes, it won't hurt to try," said Mrs. Huggins, "but don't be too disappointed if you don't get a bicycle."

"And I can go with you, can't I?" asked Beezus eagerly.

"Well . . ." Henry didn't want to bother with Beezus. He wanted to go early and look the bicycles over. If he could get a good one, he would ride it in the Rose Festival parade in a couple of weeks and really show it off.

"Of course you may go, Beezus," said Mrs. Huggins. "Henry will be glad to take you."

"Isn't it pretty far for Ramona to walk?" asked Henry. "It's about ten blocks. Long blocks, too."

"Oh, no. Ramona never gets tired," said Beezus. "Daddy says he wishes sometimes she would, but she never does. Come on, Ramona. See you in the morning, Henry." Gnawing on their cabbage cores, the girls left.

"Aw, Mom," said Henry, "why did you have to go and say they could come with me? I don't want to drag a couple of girls around all morning."

"Now, Henry," said his mother firmly, "Beezus was nice enough to come and tell you about the auction, and it won't hurt you to let her go with you."

"Oh, all right," muttered Henry.

"Why, Henry, you and Beezus used to play together so nicely. Don't you like her any more?"

"She's all right, I guess. She's just a girl, is all," said Henry, thinking of the shiny red bicycle he was going to buy the next day. Maybe Beezus would forget to come.

But Beezus did not forget. The next morning after breakfast Henry found the two girls sitting on the front steps waiting for him. When Henry and Ribsy came out of the house, Beezus started down the walk. Ramona stood still until Beezus went back and made a winding motion behind her little sister. Then Ramona walked along beside her.

"She's pretending she has to be wound up like

a toy before she can walk, and I forgot to wind her," explained Beezus.

Henry groaned. Girls thought of the dumbest things. He tried to keep ahead of them so people wouldn't think they were walking together. Ribsy trotted beside him.

"Henry Huggins, you wait for us!" said Beezus. "Your mother said we could go with you and if you don't wait I'll tell on you."

"Well, come on then," answered Henry crossly, anxious for a glimpse of that red bicycle before anyone else got there.

Suddenly Ramona stopped. Beezus wound her up again and they went on. "She ran down," explained Beezus.

Girls! Henry was disgusted. It seemed to him that it had taken half the morning to go three blocks. He saw a couple of other boys walking in the same direction, and he wondered if they were going to the auction too. He began to walk faster.

Then Henry saw Mrs. Wisser, a friend of his mother's, coming toward him. The sight of three more boys coming along on the other side of the street made Henry hope she wouldn't stop him long.

"Well, if it isn't Henry Huggins," she exclaimed. "And Beatrice."

"Hello, Mrs. Wisser," said Henry and Beezus politely.

"My, Henry, how you have grown! And you're getting to look more like your father every day. I was telling your mother only yesterday that every time I see you, you look more like your father."

Another boy hurried down the street. Was every boy in town going to the auction? Henry smiled as politely as he could at Mrs. Wisser and looked uneasily in the direction of the police station. The best bikes would be gone, he was sure, by the time he got there. Maybe he could find an older bike that just needed a little paint or something. He had plenty of time before the parade to fix it up. He tried not to show how impatient he felt.

"Don't you think he looks more like his father every day?" asked Mrs. Wisser of Beezus.

"Yes, I guess he does," said Beezus. She had also noticed the boys going in the direction of the police station, but she felt she should say something. "Especially the way his hair sticks up," she added.

Henry gave her a disgusted look.

"And is this Ribsy?" asked Mrs. Wisser. "Nice doggie."

Ribsy sat down and scratched. Thump, thump, thump went his hind leg on the sidewalk

"And this must be Ramona. How are you, sweetheart?"

Ramona was silent.

"What a pretty dress you're wearing," said Mrs. Wisser. "And it has a pocket, too. Do you have something in your pocket?"

"Yes," said Ramona.

"Isn't she sweet?" said Mrs. Wisser to Beezus. "What do you have in your little pocket, dear?"

Ramona poked her fist into her pocket and pulled out a fat slimy garden slug, which she held out to Mrs. Wisser.

"Oh," gasped Mrs. Wisser. "Oh!"

"Ramona, throw that thing away," ordered Beezus.

Henry couldn't help grinning, Mrs. Wisser looked so horrified.

"Well . . . I must be running along," said Mrs. Wisser.

"Good-by, Mrs. Wisser," said Beezus and Henry. Ramona put her slug back in her pocket, Beezus wound her up again, and they went on.

Until they reached the Glenwood shopping district, Henry almost thought girls were good for something after all. Then Ramona stopped in front of the Supermarket. "I'm hungry," she announced.

"Come on, Ramona," coaxed Beezus. "We're in a hurry."

"I'm hungry," repeated Ramona.

Henry groaned. He knew they couldn't go any

farther until Ramona had something to eat. That was the kind of little girl she was.

"I have a quarter," said Beezus. "I better get her something."

"O.K.," agreed Henry reluctantly. "I could stand something myself." Then Henry noticed a sign on the door of the market. It said *No dogs allowed in food stores.*

"Lie down, Ribsy," he ordered, as he went through the swinging door.

On the next swing of the door Ribsy came in too. "Sorry, sonny," said a clerk. "You'll have to take your dog outside."

"Beat it," said Henry to his dog. Ribsy sat down. "Come on, you old dog," said Henry, seizing his pet by the collar and dragging him out onto the sidewalk.

Henry hurried back into the market and was trying to decide between a bag of Cheezy Chips and a box of Fig Newtons when the clerk said,

"Say, sonny, I thought I told you to get that dog out of here."

Once more Henry dragged Ribsy out. This time he dug into his pocket and pulled out a piece of heavy twine. He tied one end to Ribsy's collar and fastened the other end securely to a parking meter. "Now don't you chew the twine," he said, before he went back into the store. He chose the Cheezy Chips and stood impatiently behind Beezus in line at the cashier's counter.

Finally they were out on the sidewalk again, where they found Ribsy busy chewing the twine. Beezus had to stop and find several lions in the animal-cracker box she had bought, because Ramona wanted to eat all the lions first. Henry felt it was pretty useless to try to go any place with a couple of girls. But maybe he would get there in time to find a bike in fairly good condition with just a few spokes missing.

"Hey, Henry!" It was Robert calling.

Henry, who was trying to untie Ribsy from the parking meter, saw Scooter pedaling his bicycle slowly down the sidewalk while Robert jogged along at his side.

"Bet you're going to the bike sale," said Scooter. "We're going just to watch."

"What's that paper under Ribsy's collar?" asked Robert.

"What paper?" said Henry. Sure enough, there *was* a paper under Ribsy's collar. Henry pulled it out and unfolded it as the other children crowded around.

Scooter was first to understand. He shouted with laughter. "It's a parking ticket. Ribsy got a parking ticket!"

The children all laughed. "Don't be dumb," said Henry. "Everybody knows dogs don't get parking tickets."

"Sure it's a ticket," said Scooter. "See, it says *Notice of traffic violation* across the top, and *vio-*

lation means he's done something wrong, doesn't it?"

"Did you put a penny in the meter?" asked Robert.

"That's right. Did you put a penny in the meter when you parked your dog?" laughed Scooter.

"I didn't know leaving a dog on the sidewalk counted as parking," said Henry, looking at the meter. "See! The red thing doesn't show and there's still sixteen minutes left from whoever put the money in before."

"Maybe there was a car here and Ribsy got a ticket for double parking," said Scooter, guffawing again.

Beezus handed Ramona another lion. "That's all the lions. You'll have to eat camels now." Then she said to Henry, "Maybe it was a mistake."

"How could it be a mistake?" asked Scooter. "It was under Ribsy's collar, wasn't it?" He looked at the ticket again. "See, it says here that you have violated a code. The policeman has written the number of the law you broke. I know, because my dad explained it to me once when he got a ticket. Maybe you have to put in more money to park dogs."

"Maybe they'll put Ribsy in jail," suggested Robert.

"No they won't," said Henry. "You never heard of them putting a car in jail, did you? This is the same thing."

"That's right," agreed Scooter, and laughed. "Maybe they'll put you in jail."

"What do you suppose they'll do, Henry?" asked Beezus anxiously.

"I don't know. I guess I'll have to pay a fine." Henry stuffed the ticket in his pocket.

"My dad knows a man who knows the mayor," said Robert. "Maybe he could do something about it."

"No, I'll have to take it out of my bike money," said Henry. "Say, Scoot, how much did your dad pay when he got the ticket?"

"A dollar, I think," said Scooter. "No, I guess it was two."

There went at least a dollar from Henry's bike fund. Maybe two. Two dollars plus a dime for Cheezy Chips. Take that from four dollars and fourteen cents and he had two dollars and four cents left for a bike—that is, if he ever got to the auction and if there were any bikes left when he did get there. Maybe he could get a good sturdy frame and pick up a couple of wheels some place.

"You could ask at the police station," suggested Beezus.

Why hadn't he thought of that before? "Hey, kids, let's go," said Henry. He didn't have to untie the twine. Ribsy had chewed it in two.

Scooter pedaled slowly and the others ran along

beside him. Even Ramona ran. Eating all the lions out of the animal-cracker box made her forget she had to be wound up.

Henry worried about the ticket. What was wrong with leaving Ribsy outside the Supermarket? He couldn't take him in, so he had to leave him out, didn't he? And if he didn't tie him, he wouldn't stay out, would he? It must be a mistake. It had to be. If only he could get to the station and find out before the auction.

"Wow!" exclaimed Henry, when they finally turned a corner and came to the Glenwood police station. The steps of the building swarmed with children. The driveway beside the station was crammed with boys and girls, and grownups, and dogs, too. Other children perched on the fence between the driveway and the apartment house on the other side. More children were getting out of the cars that jammed the streets.

"I'll go with you to see about the ticket," Beezus

told Henry. Scooter and Robert decided they would try to find a place on the fence.

When Henry made his way through the crowd on the steps, he found a policeman blocking the door. "Around to the side of the building, kids," he said. "The auction is out in the driveway and no one is allowed to go through the station."

"But I just wanted to ask . . ." said Henry.

"Run along, everybody," directed the policeman.

"But . . ." said Henry.

"Sorry," said the policeman.

"Come on." Beezus tugged at Henry's sleeve. "It's started already. You can ask afterward."

"But I won't know how much money I can spend," protested Henry, as he followed Beezus. When they reached the driveway, Henry tried to worm his way through the crowd. Maybe he could get to the back door of the police station and ask about his ticket there.

"Hey, quit shoving," ordered a boy.

"Yes, we were here first," said another. "Who do you think you are?"

"We'll never make it to the back door in time. There must be other policemen around some place." Henry was worried, because he could hear the auctioneer's voice and knew that bicycles were being sold.

"What am I bid for this bicycle?" Henry heard faintly above the noise of the crowd. He knew he had to get his ticket straightened out pretty soon, or he might as well go home and forget the whole thing.

"There's a policeman," exclaimed Beezus. "Over there by the fence."

When Henry, the two girls, and Ribsy had fought their way through the crowd to the policeman, they found he was too busy trying to get boys off the fence to notice them.

Henry didn't know how to speak to an officer.

"Mr. . . . uh . . . Policeman," he said cautiously.

"All right, boys," directed the man. "Down off the fence."

The auctioneer's voice continued. "Sold!" he shouted.

Henry and Beezus exchanged anxious looks. There went another bike. "Mr. Policeman!" This time Henry spoke louder.

Still the officer did not hear.

Then Ramona marched over to him and tugged at the leg of his uniform. "Hey!" she yelled.

Surprised, the officer looked down at her. "Hello there. Something I can do for you?" he asked.

"Yes." Henry spoke up. "Uh . . . this is my dog, Ribsy."

"How do you do, Ribsy," said the puzzled policeman.

Ribsy sat down and held out his paw, the right

NOTICE

one, too. The officer shook it. Henry was glad to see his dog do the correct thing for once.

"He . . . uh . . . well, he got a parking ticket," said Henry.

"He what?" The policeman sounded baffled.

Henry pulled the crumpled ticket out of his pocket. "He got a parking ticket," he repeated. "I can't understand it. He wasn't double parked. There was money in the meter and there wasn't any car by it." Then he explained about Ramona being hungry and Ribsy following him into the market.

The policeman looked at the ticket and began to smile. Then he laughed. A couple of other officers came to see what he was laughing at. They laughed too. Henry felt uncomfortable and wondered if he had said the wrong thing.

"Did you never hear that it is against the law to tie anything to a parking meter?" the first officer finally asked.

So that was it! "No, sir," said Henry politely. "I just tied him with a thin piece of twine. It wasn't a big rope or anything."

Chuckling, the policeman put the ticket in his pocket and patted Ribsy's head. "Well . . . since you didn't know about the law, I'll see what I can do about this. But from now on you'd better find some place else to park your dog."

"Gee, thanks," said Henry gratefully. "Thanks millions." Ribsy held out his paw again.

What a relief! Now Henry could bid four dollars and fourteen cents for a bicycle. No, four dollars and four cents. He had spent a dime on Cheezy Chips. "Come on, Beezus," Henry said. "Let's get in there and start bidding!"

CHAPTER FIVE

Beezus Makes a Bid

HENRY, Ribsy, and the two girls struggled into the mob on the driveway. Sometimes they moved ahead a foot, sometimes an inch, but most of the time they stood still. It seemed to Henry that a lot of awfully big people stepped on his toes. The children could barely hear the auctioneer above the noise of the crowd. "What am I bid for bicycle Number Seven?" the man was shouting.

Henry jumped as high as he could to see the bicycle.

"Quit jumping on my toes," said the boy behind him.

Ribsy yelped. "You keep off my dog's tail," Henry said to another boy. He wondered how much he dared bid. Should he start with fifty cents or should he bid four dollars and four cents all at once and hope no one else had that much money?

"I'm hungry," yelled Ramona.

Beezus rummaged in the box of animal crackers. "Here's an elephant," she offered. "You've eaten all the lions and camels."

"No!" screamed Ramona. "I don't like elephants."

Henry was disgusted. "Don't be dumb," he said, wondering if Ramona would ever give him a chance to bid. "All animal crackers taste alike."

"I don't *like* elephants," Ramona screamed again, looking as if she were going to cry.

"Oh, all right." Beezus pawed through the box again. "Here's a monkey." To Henry's relief, Ramona ate the monkey.

It seemed as if everyone were waving his hand and shouting a number at the auctioneer.

"Two dollars!" yelled the boy behind Henry.

"Ten cents!" shouted someone in front of him.

"A penny," screamed a little girl.

"A million dollars," sang out Scooter, who was still on the fence.

"Two million," bid another.

"Quiet, everybody!" roared the auctioneer, mopping his face with his handkerchief. "I've been in this business twenty years, and I've never seen anything like this. We have fifty items to sell and we don't want to take all day. We don't have time for any funny business. Now, how much am

I bid for this bicycle? One dollar from the boy on the fence . . . a dollar and a quarter, a dollar and a half, two dollars from the boy in the red sweater . . . five dollars. Five dollars once, five dollars twice . . . six dollars."

Only fifty items, when the paper had said a hundred! It seemed to Henry that his chance of getting a bicycle was growing smaller by the minute.

"A million dollars," yelled Scooter again.

The auctioneer glared at him and continued. "Six dollars once . . . six dollars twice . . . bicycle Number Seven sold to the boy in the green sweater for six dollars!"

"Aw, it wasn't any good, anyway," Henry heard someone say. "It had only one wheel."

Six dollars for a bike with one wheel! "I wonder how much a bike with two wheels is going to cost," Henry said to Beezus.

"Maybe the people with the most money will

get bicycles and go home, and then the kids who haven't much will have a chance," suggested Beezus.

"I guess I'll stick around and see," said Henry. The next item the auctioneer held up was a Taylor-tot. Henry was disgusted. The paper hadn't said anything about Taylor-tots.

"Stop fussing, Ramona," said Beezus. "I know you can't see anything, but pretty soon Henry will get a bike and we can go home."

Ramona began to pound Ribsy's back with her fist. The dog looked around for a way to escape, but there were too many people.

"Cut it out, Ramona," ordered Henry.

Then a strange woman standing behind Henry spoke. "No, no, little girl. Mustn't hit the doggie. *Love* the doggie."

Ramona stared at the woman. Then she threw both arms around Ribsy's neck and squeezed as hard as she could. Ribsy struggled.

"Hey, you're choking him," objected Henry, as Beezus pried her little sister loose from the dog.

"I want to go home," said Ramona.

"After while," answered Beezus crossly.

Henry saw that he had better start bidding on a bike. If Ramona wanted to go home, they would probably have to go home. Next a bicycle was sold to a boy who bellowed, "Seven dollars and sixty-four cents!" A battered tricycle went for a dollar. Another bicycle sold for five dollars to a boy who got his friends to yell with him, so he could be heard above the crowd. The boy behind Beezus had bid seven dollars, but the auctioneer didn't hear.

Henry saw that, with so many people shouting and waving their hands and the auctioneer trying to sell the bicycles as fast as he could, it was more important for a boy to make himself heard above the crowd than to have a lot of money to spend.

If only there were some way he could make the auctioneer hear him! Henry jumped as high as he could for a glimpse of the next bicycle. The handle bars were missing, but he was sure that if he got it, he could find a pair of old handle bars somewhere. "One dollar!" he yelled at the top of his voice. His words were lost in a chorus of bids.

"I'll help you yell," said Beezus.

"Two dollars!" they shouted together. The auctioneer did not hear them.

Just then there was a lull in the noise of the crowd and Ramona's voice rang out. "I'm going to throw up," she announced.

Instantly everyone standing near her managed to move a few inches away. Ribsy used the extra space to sit down and scratch.

"Beezus, don't just stand there. Do something." Henry was thoroughly alarmed. Leave it to Ramona to get sick just when he had figured out the way the auction worked.

Beezus calmly handed Ramona another animal cracker. "Oh, don't pay any attention to her," she said.

The lady behind Henry tapped Beezus on the shoulder and asked, "Don't you think you had better take your little sister home?"

"She's all right. She just says that when she wants her own way," Beezus explained. "Come on, Henry, I'll help you yell again."

"I'm going to throw up," screamed Ramona.

Henry was relieved that Ramona was really all right, even if he had missed another chance to bid. The lady was not so sure. Again she tapped Beezus on the shoulder. "I think you'd better take your sister home. Maybe she isn't feeling well."

Ramona beamed. Beezus and Henry exchanged unhappy looks. It looked as if Ramona was going to get her own way. She usually did.

"Come with me," said the lady firmly. "I'll help you through the crowd."

"Honestly, she's all right," protested Beezus. "She's just saying that."

"She's O.K.," agreed Henry. "Beezus knows." There must be some way to keep Ramona from getting her own way.

The lady did not seem to hear. "Take my hand, little girl," she said, as if she meant to be obeyed. "Come on, children." The people who were standing near them were still eying Ramona uneasily and were glad to make a path to let them through.

Why couldn't the lady leave them alone? Henry didn't see how he could bear to move away from the auctioneer, when it had been such hard work to get through the crowd. For a minute he thought he wouldn't leave. If he let Beezus and Ramona go alone, maybe he would get a chance to bid. Still, his mother said he had to take Beezus with him, so maybe they'd better stay together. He didn't want to catch it when he got home.

"Will you let us through, please? This little girl isn't feeling well," the lady repeated. The crowd, pleased to see that someone was leaving, let them through. Henry begrudged every step that took them away from the auctioneer.

At last they reached the sidewalk. "There you are," said the lady cheerfully. "Run along now and tell your mother she had better put your little sister to bed." Then she turned and made her way back into the crowd.

There they were, all right. Disgusted, Henry turned on Ramona. "Now see what you've done. How am I going to bid on a bike when we can't even hear the auctioneer way out here?"

"I want to go home," said Ramona.

"Don't you want Henry to get a bicycle?" asked Beezus.

"No," said Ramona.

Beezus grabbed her little sister by the hand.

"Ramona Geraldine Quimby," she snapped, "you're coming with us and you're going to behave yourself!"

"Yes," agreed Henry. "I'm pretty tired of being pushed around by a little kid like you."

Beezus glared at her sister. "And if you don't behave I'll . . . I'll tell Mother about the time you waited until she went to the store and then tried to give the cat a bath in the Bendix. Then you'll be sorry!"

Ramona sulked but she didn't say anything. Wearily the children struggled into the crowd. Ribsy's tail drooped. Henry was so hot and tired he felt it was pretty useless to go back at all. Ramona would probably think of something else, anyway. By staying on the edge of the driveway and squeezing along the edge of the police station, they moved slowly ahead.

At last they were able to hear the auctioneer again. Henry was afraid there were so many tall people in front of them that they couldn't be seen even if they could make themselves heard. Beezus and Henry yelled experimentally a couple of times, but they really didn't expect to be heard.

"I wish Robert and Scooter were here," said Henry. "Maybe if we all yelled together he would hear us."

"They're on the other side of the driveway," said Beezus. "We could never get through." Then, looking frantically around, she gasped, "Ramona! Where's Ramona? I can't find her."

"Maybe she went home." Henry looked around, but it was impossible to see more than a few feet in any direction.

"She was down here with Ribsy a minute ago." Beezus looked frightened. "Henry, what will Mother say if I've lost her for keeps?"

"She must be around some place. She couldn't go far in this crowd." Henry was disgusted. First it was a parking ticket on a dog, because Ramona was hungry. Then because of her they were taken out of the crowd. And now she had to wander off when he was trying to bid on a bike. That's what happened when he tried to go some place with a couple of girls. Nevertheless, he looked around for Beezus' little sister while the bidding continued.

"Where can she be?" Beezus was frantic. "Maybe she's kidnaped."

Jeepers, thought Henry. I hope she isn't going to cry. He had enough troubles without Beezus crying all over the place. He knew Ramona couldn't be far away, and he was sure no one would ever kidnap her. Especially not if they knew her. Now all he had to do was find her before the auction ended.

"If we went up in front, we could ask the auctioneer to ask about her," suggested Henry. He didn't mention that his chances of bidding would also be better.

"Have you seen my little sister?" Beezus asked the people around her.

Henry inquired if anyone had seen a little girl in a blue dress, but no one had noticed her.

"What are we going to do, Henry?" asked Beezus, blinking her eyes to keep back the tears. "I can't go home without her. I've got to find her. I've got to."

Then the auctioneer pounded his gavel and roared, "Quiet, everybody!" The crowd was almost silent. "Has someone lost a little girl?" He held Ramona up for everyone to see. Her face was streaked with tears and she clutched her slug in one hand.

"One dollar!" yelled Scooter.

"Quiet!" shouted the auctioneer.

"It's Ramona!" Beezus cried out. "It's my little sister."

"Will you come up and get your sister?" asked the auctioneer. "Make way for the little lady to come for her sister."

Hey, thought Henry, here's my chance. I'll go with her and get up in front where the auctioneer can see me and then maybe he can hear me bid. The people in front moved aside to let Beezus through. Henry started after her.

"Where do you think you're going?" the big boy in front of Henry demanded.

"With her," said Henry.

"You're not going to get ahead of me," said another boy.

By that time the path the crowd had made for Beezus closed up again. Henry couldn't let his one chance at a bicycle get away from him. "Beezus," he called desperately, "if you see a good bike, bid for me. Four dollars and four cents."

"O.K.," Beezus answered through the crowd.

The auction continued. In spite of other people's toes, Henry jumped as high as he could each time a bicycle was held up. If Beezus could make the auctioneer hear, it might be his. Two bicycles went by. Henry grew more and more uneasy, waiting to hear a shout of "Four dollars and four cents!" Beezus must be in the very front row. Why didn't she bid? What had gone wrong?

Then the auctioneer's voice rang out. "Sold for four dollars and four cents! Bicycle Number Thirty-two sold to the little lady who lost her sister."

Beezus had bid!

Joyfully Henry sprang into the air to see his bike. He couldn't see a thing, but that was all right. There was a bicycle waiting for him. A bike of his very own.

After that Henry lost interest in the auction. He was busy wondering what his bicycle looked like. He hoped it was red and had a horn and a light. Gradually the crowd began to leave, and Henry and his dog were able to work their way up to the front where Beezus and Ramona were waiting.

Beezus, who was holding a place in the line of people paying for bicycles, looked pleased and excited. "Henry, I got you a real good one with wheels and handle bars and everything. It's in that pile. I had the man write your name on the tag."

Henry took his place in line, and was trying to guess which bicycle in the heap was his when Robert and Scooter joined him.

32

"Did you find out about the ticket?" asked Robert.

"Sure, and I got a bike, too," boasted Henry.

"Yeah?" Scooter plainly did not believe him.

"Yes. And I'm not going to jail or anything, either." Then Henry explained about the policeman and the ticket.

"I bet the bike isn't any good," remarked Scooter.

"It is too a good bike," Beezus contradicted. "It has two wheels and everything. Of course it isn't exactly new, but it's a good bike just the same. You wait and see."

"Sure, it's a good bike if Beezus says so," Henry bragged. "You just wait until I ride it in the Rose Festival parade."

Gradually the line moved forward. "Number Thirty-two," said Henry, when his turn came. At last he nearly had his hands on his very own bike. He had had to run along the sidewalk beside

Scooter on the way to the auction, but he was going to ride his own bike home. He counted out the four dollars and four cents.

"There'll be something wrong with it. You just wait and see," said Scooter.

"There will not," said Beezus. "At least not anything important."

The officer finally untangled Henry's bicycle from the rest of the pile.

Scooter and Robert began to howl with laughter. Henry groaned. What could you expect when you went to an auction with a girl? The bicycle had two wheels and handle bars all right, but there was something else wrong with it. It was a girl's bicycle.

CHAPTER SIX

Henry's Bargain Bike

HENRY was so disappointed he could hardly bear it. He could never ride a girl's bike in the Rose Festival parade.

Beezus was right. The bicycle did have two wheels and handle bars. It did not, however, have a lot of other things. There was no air in the tires and very little paint on the frame. Spokes were missing, and because there was no graphite on the chain, the pedals made a groaning noise when they were pushed around. But most important of all, the bicycle did not have a bar from the seat to the handle bars. If only there were some way to turn it into a boy's bike, the rest would be easy. With a few repairs, a coat of paint, and some paper trimming, it would be good enough to ride in the parade.

Henry sighed and started to push his bicycle home.

"I'm sorry, Henry," said Beezus. "After some of the other bikes it looked pretty good, and I didn't think about it being a girl's bike."

"Aw, that's all right," muttered Henry. He supposed it wasn't really her fault. He couldn't expect a girl to know anything about bicycles.

"Maybe you could find a girl who has a boy's bike and make a trade," suggested Beezus.

Henry thought this over. "The trouble is, girls ride boys' bikes, but boys won't ride girls' bikes. If I found a girl who had a boy's bike, she'd probably want to keep it." He pushed his bicycle in silence for a while and then said, "I'll just have to fix it someway, that's all."

After lunch Henry made a quick trip to the Rose City Bike and Trike Shop. His mother had given him the money for the twenty-two new spokes he needed. The man in the shop explained to Henry how to put new spokes into the wheels.

As Henry left the shop, he could not help noticing a shiny new bike with a racy red frame and a built-in headlight. If only his bicycle looked like that!

Back home, Henry went to work on his bicycle in his back yard. First he slipped off the tires and removed the broken spokes with his father's pliers. Then he poked one end of each new spoke into its hole in the hub and the other end into the rim.

Henry was tightening the nuts that held the spokes in place when Beezus and Ramona came up the driveway. Beezus was carrying her baton and Ramona was riding her shiny new tricycle. The spokes in her wheels glistened in the sunshine as she pedaled along beside Beezus. When she got off the tricycle, she leaned it on two wheels against the house as if it were a bicycle.

"Your bike looks better already," said Beezus, who was anxious to have Henry's bicycle turn out right after her mistake that morning.

Henry tugged the tires back over the rims. "Yes, but not much," he said. "Now I've got to find a way to turn it into a boy's bike."

At least, it does have a parking stand, thought Henry, as he propped the bike up.

He and Beezus studied it. "If I had a pipe and some welding stuff and knew how to weld, I could weld a pipe across to make it into a boy's bike," observed Henry.

"It would be easier to tie a piece of broom handle across," said Beezus.

Henry frowned. Girls always thought of the dumbest things. Still, it might work—at least until he could think of a better idea. "O.K., I'll give it a try," he said.

Henry found an old broom handle in the basement, measured it carefully, and sawed it off on the mark he had made. Then, with a piece of twine he happened to have in his pocket, he tied one end of the handle under the seat. The other he fastened below the handle bars.

Henry stood back to look at his work. Well, it could be better. Maybe if he painted the bike and the broom handle the same color and rode fast, nobody would notice. And, for the parade, he could cover the broom handle with roses or crepe paper or something.

"That looks keen," said Beezus, twirling her baton around her fingers. "It's good enough to ride in the Rose Festival parade."

"Well . . . maybe." Henry thought he'd better make sure he could fix his bicycle before he said anything more about the parade. Last year he had been a snake charmer with a bath-towel turban on his head and a snake made out of a stuffed nylon stocking around his neck, but this year he was getting pretty old to wear a costume and walk. He was determined to get his bike fixed in time.

Henry was examining the tires for holes when Robert came up the driveway.

"What have you got that piece of broom handle tied to the bike for?" demanded Robert.

Henry didn't answer. Robert knew very well why the handle was tied to the bike.

"You just wait," said Beezus, flipping her baton. "Henry's bike is going to look all right when he gets it painted. He's going to ride it in the parade."

"I didn't say for sure," protested Henry, relieved that at least there were no visible holes in the tires.

"I bet you do." Beezus twirled the baton over her head. This time she dropped it.

"Boi-i-ing!" shouted Robert. Henry was too busy with his bike to notice what was going on.

"Oh, be quiet!" snapped Beezus, as she picked

up the baton. "You just wait until I twirl my baton in the parade. Mother is going to make me a drum-majorette costume."

"The parade is only two weeks away." Robert twanged a spoke with his finger. "You'll have to be a whole lot better than that. And anyway, where will you get a band to lead?"

"You don't have to have a band." Beezus tried to flip her baton behind her back but dropped it in the grass. "I'm just going to march and twirl. Mary Jane is going to wear her rosebud costume and make a wreath of roses for Patsy to wear around her neck." Patsy was Mary Jane's cocker spaniel.

"I'm going to be the hind legs of a giraffe," said Robert. "A fellow I know on Thirty-third Street is going to be the front half."

"Bet you come apart in the middle," said Beezus, who had once been the front end of a horse in a park circus.

Robert examined the bicycle carefully while Henry plucked at each spoke to see if it were tight enough. Some were tight, but many were loose. "Wish I had a real spoke wrench," muttered Henry. "Now I'll have to take the tires off again."

"Scooter has a wrench in that little kit he carries on his bike," said Robert. "I've seen him use it. It's a thing that fits around the end of the spoke that goes through the rim."

"You watch Ramona. I'll go ask Scooter if you can borrow it," said Beezus, anxious to help. She ran down the driveway before Henry could object. He didn't want to borrow Scooter's wrench, because Scooter might decide to come over and see what he was doing.

"Hey, Ramona, stop pulling Ribsy's ears," ordered Henry. "Why don't you play you're waiting for a bus?"

"O.K.," was Ramona's surprising answer, as she sat down on the back steps.

When Beezus returned with the wrench, Henry went to work on the spokes. He went around both wheels and tightened each spoke. Then he went over them again and gave them an extra twist just to make sure. He wasn't going to have any loose spokes on his bike.

"Come on, Robert, give me a hand," Henry said, after he had found a tire pump in the garage. He was beginning to feel excited. In a few minutes he could try his bike. The boys fitted the rubber tube over the valve on the rim and were taking turns pumping, when Scooter came up the driveway.

"Hi!" said Henry. He wondered what Scooter, who knew a lot about bicycles, would say.

Scooter laughed. "What have you got that old broom handle tied to the frame for?"

Henry, who was beginning to be sensitive about that broom handle, went on pumping.

Scooter walked around the bike and studied it

carefully. He tried the bell, which *pinged* feebly. He wiggled the seat and examined the chain. There was no doubt about it. Scooter was an expert on bicycles.

Henry waited anxiously for the expert's opinion. Except for that broom handle, he secretly thought his bike was pretty good now that the spokes were in. He paused in his pumping to ask, "Not bad for four dollars and four cents, is it?"

Scooter jiggled the handle bars. He ran his finger over the tires.

Henry began to feel uneasy. "Of course," he added, "I still have a lot of things to do to it. Paint it and stuff."

Scooter examined the fork that held the front wheel. He examined the fork that held the back wheel.

Old show-off, thought Henry. Why doesn't he say something?

"Well . . ." said Scooter at last, "I suppose it

will do for a kid your age. Of course, it needs a lot of work before it'll be safe to use. You'll need a light and a reflector and a good bell. The handle bars are loose and you need another handle grip. You'll have to get a chain guard, and have both forks straightened, and tighten the seat, and mend the right pedal, and let's see . . . Those tires are pretty smooth, and I don't like the looks of that brake."

Discouraged, Henry stared at his bike. Except for the missing handle grip and the bell, he hadn't noticed any of the things Scooter mentioned. Leave it to Scooter to find a lot of things wrong. And the worst of it was, Scooter was probably right.

Henry went on pumping. "Well, one thing at a time," he said, because he couldn't think of anything else to say.

"Say, Huggins," said Scooter. "I've got an idea how we could win a blue ribbon in the bicycle section of the parade after you do some more work on your bike."

"How?" asked Henry.

"Let's take the front wheel off that old bike and fasten the front fork to the back wheel of my bike and make a tandem. You know, a bicycle built for two, only ours will have three wheels."

"Will it really work?" Robert was impressed with the suggestion.

"Sure it'll work," said Scooter. "How about it, Huggins?"

Henry was impressed with the idea too, but he didn't want to ride in the parade on an old piece of a bike fastened to Scooter's good bike. Not after the way Scooter had acted. "Nope. I'm going to do something else," he announced.

"Aw, come on," said Scooter. "Don't you think it's a good idea?"

"Sure, it's a good idea," Henry had to admit. "I'm just going to do something else, is all."

"What?" demanded Robert.

"I bet you think you're going to ride that bike," said Scooter.

"What if I am?" asked Henry. "You just wait. I'll get it all fixed up and trimmed with flowers and things, and nobody'll know it's an old bike I got at an auction."

"Let's see you ride it," said Scooter, when at last the tires were hard.

"O.K. I suppose you think I can't." Just for good measure, Henry gave several spokes an extra hard twist with the wrench.

His mouth was dry as he kicked the parking stand into place. He knew the bicycle would wobble at first, and he didn't want to take a spill in front of everyone. He wheeled the bicycle to the driveway, stepped on the pedal, and threw his leg over the seat. When his foot found the other pedal, he discovered that something was terribly wrong. There was no pull to the pedals. His feet

spun around helplessly. Because the driveway sloped, he was able to coast, wobbling from side to side. Barking furiously, Ribsy ran along beside him.

Henry's ears burned when he heard his audience shriek with laughter. Suddenly the pedals caught, and he was able to use them. Then he realized there was something else wrong with his bicycle. It moved with a peculiar twisting motion that made Henry go up and down as if he were on a rocking horse. The chain, which still had no graphite on it, groaned. Up and down he bobbed as he struggled to keep his balance. Then, in the midst of his confusion, he saw that the front wheel was so bent that it was no longer round. The back wheel must be bent, too, because he could hear it scraping against the fender every time it went around.

The two boys and Beezus, screaming with laughter, ran along behind Henry. Suddenly the groaning of the chain stopped, and he found his feet spinning helplessly on the pedals.

"Ride 'em, cowboy!" shouted Scooter, as Henry coasted on the twisting bicycle and pumped the spinning pedals furiously in his effort to make them work again.

The bicycle was wobbling out of control. Henry frantically tried to apply the coaster brake. Instead of stopping, the pedals began to spin backwards. Henry tried to stop by dragging his foot, but the leg of his jeans caught in the chain. The bicycle spilled him onto the sidewalk and toppled over on top of him.

The others laughed even harder.

Henry worked his jeans out of the chain, untangled himself from the bike, and stood up, scowling and rubbing himself. "All right, cut it out. You're not funny!" he said to Robert and Scooter, who were pounding each other on the back and whooping with laughter.

"That coaster brake . . ." Scooter was laughing so hard he couldn't go on.

"And those wheels!" howled Robert.

Scooter doubled up with laughter. "It's the spokes," he whooped. "Who tightened them for you? Whoever it was sure bent the wheels doing it."

"I did it myself," said Henry with dignity, wondering if he hadn't broken a few bones. As he started to wheel the bicycle up the driveway, he was glad to see that Beezus was no longer laughing at him.

"Are you still going to ride it in the parade?" asked Scooter.

"No," said Henry coldly. He wheeled his bike into the garage, came out, and closed the doors. "I hope you're satisfied, Scooter McCarthy," he said crossly.

Scooter stopped laughing. "Say, Huggins, if I help you straighten out that back wheel, how about riding in the parade like I said?"

"No thanks," said Henry, patting Ribsy's head. Good old Ribsy. At least he had one friend left.

"Aw, come on," coaxed Scooter.

"Nope," said Henry flatly.

"O.K., if that's the way you feel," said Scooter, shrugging his shoulders. "Come on, Robert. Help me roll my *Journals.*"

As the two boys left, Henry threw himself down on the back steps.

Beezus sat beside him. "I've got an idea," she said. "Why don't you wear a clown suit and ride the bike in the parade, and everybody will think you meant to be funny."

Henry plucked a blade of grass. "No, I guess not. I'll think of something." He blew on the grass, which made a sputtering noise. Well, anyway, Beezus wasn't laughing at him, and he probably would think of something. Maybe his mother would help him with a costume. It wouldn't be the same as riding a bike, though.

Beezus, seeing that Henry wanted to be alone, decided it was time to go home. Henry was silent as he watched Ramona mount her shiny tricycle and ride off, her spokes twinkling in the sunshine.

He continued to sit and make sputtering noises on the blade of grass.

Mrs. Huggins came out and sat on the steps beside Henry. "I was watching through the window," she said.

Henry didn't say anything. Probably everyone on Klickitat Street was watching.

"I'm sorry we can't get you a new bicycle, Henry," said his mother, "but I think we could manage twenty dollars for a second-hand bicycle. If we watched the classified ads in the paper, we might find a good one that someone wanted to sell."

Henry sighed. "Gee, thanks a lot, Mom, but I guess not. If I can't have a brand-new bike without a single thing wrong with it, I guess I can get along without one."

Mrs. Huggins smiled. "I understand. When I was your age I wanted some brand-new ice skates attached to white shoes. But I had to use my brother's old hockey skates, so I know just how you feel." She patted Henry lightly on the shoulder and went back into the house.

Somehow, Henry found he felt more cheerful. He blew on the blade of grass and produced an ear-splitting whistle. He sat on the steps blowing and whistling and thinking about the shiny red bicycle in the Rose City Bike and Trike Shop.

CHAPTER SEVEN

The Boy Who Ate Dog Food

THE next Friday afternoon Henry and Ribsy were walking home from school. They were going the long way past the Rose City Bike and Trike Shop so Henry could look at what he had come to think of as his bicycle—the one with the racy red frame and the built-in headlight. The only thing wrong with it was the price—fifty-nine dollars and ninety-five cents. It was exactly what Henry wanted, and he looked at it every time he had a chance.

After making sure his bike was still in the shop, Henry moved on. He was still trying to think of

something he could do in the Rose Festival parade. Across the street from the Supermarket he stopped to look at the new Colossal Market building that had just been finished. It covered a whole city block, and Henry had heard that the market would sell not only meats, groceries, and drugs, but would also have a filling station, a soda fountain, a florist's stand, a beauty shop, a hardware store, and almost anything else you could think of.

Today there was a huge sign across the front of the building. Henry stopped to read it. The sign said:

TONITE

GRAND OPENING

MODERN ONE-STOP SHOPPING

DE LUXE NEW COLOSSAL MARKET

NOW READY TO SERVE YOU

25 FREE DOOR PRIZES 25

FREE SAMPLES

FREE GARDENIAS FOR LADIES

FREE BALLOONS FOR KIDDIES

ENTERTAINMENT!

Jeepers, thought Henry. That's a lot of free stuff. He decided to ask his mother and father to go. It was fun to collect free samples, and his mother might like a gardenia.

Henry was still trying to think of a good idea for the parade, when he and his mother and father joined the crowd of people visiting the new market that evening. Beezus was with them, because her mother had to stay at home to put Ramona to bed. Henry had given Ribsy a big bone for dinner so he would stay in his yard. If dogs had to stay out of the Supermarket, they would certainly have to stay out of the Colossal Market.

In front of the Colossal Market six searchlights sent giant fingers of light into the sky. Henry saw Robert and Scooter talking to the men who ran the gasoline generators. As Henry and his father and mother and Beezus entered the market, someone handed each of them a ticket for the door prize. After they had written their names on the tickets and dropped them into a barrel, a girl in a fluffy blue skirt gave Mr. Huggins a package of razor blades. Another girl in a fluffy red skirt gave Mrs. Huggins a gardenia, while a clown offered Henry and Beezus balloons.

Beezus asked if she couldn't count as a lady and have a gardenia instead of a balloon. When the girl handed her the flower, she took it, closed her eyes, and breathed deeply.

"Smell it, Henry," she said. "Did you ever smell anything so beautiful in your whole life?"

Henry gave it a quick sniff. "It's all right," he said, tying the string of his balloon to the button on his beanie. When he put the beanie back on his head, he hung onto it with one hand until he was sure the balloon wouldn't carry it away.

After agreeing to meet his mother and father by the front door at eight-thirty, Henry said, "Come on, Beezus, let's find some free samples."

Sniffing her gardenia, Beezus followed Henry, who had to stop before long and untangle his balloon string from the buttons of a lady's coat. Then they sampled doughnuts, hot from a doughnut machine, and looked over the largest selection of comic books they had ever seen. They tasted frozen orange juice and decided to pass up a free sample of dehydrated Vitaveg soup in order to watch a man demonstrate a gadget for making roses out of beets and turnips. Then they paused at the Colossal Beauty Shoppe to watch a lady have a free facial. Henry thought she looked funny with her hair wrapped in a towel and greasy stuff smeared on her face. As he caught a glimpse of himself in a mirror, he decided he might wear a balloon on his beanie in the parade.

"Look!" Beezus grabbed Henry's arm and pointed to the platform where three girls from a dancing school had been tap-dancing. "The drawing for the door prizes is starting. There's the Rose Festival queen and her princesses."

As the crowd pressed toward the platform, the master of ceremonies announced that the owner of the first ticket the queen pulled from the barrel would receive, absolutely free of charge, one white side-wall tire from the Colossal Filling Station.

"Maybe you'll win it," said Beezus.

Henry wasn't sure his father needed one white side-wall tire, since all his other tires were black, so he wasn't disappointed when his name was not called. He soon lost interest in door prizes, because there were so many grownups in front of him that he couldn't see what was happening.

"Come on, Beezus," he said. "I bet this is a good time to get free samples."

They found Robert and Scooter in front of the doughnut machine. "This is my third free sample," said Scooter. "Come on, let's see what else we can find."

They tasted catsup, potato chips, jam, and cheese. Soon the pockets of Henry's jeans bulged with sample boxes and bottles of Oatsies, Glit, and 3-Minit Whisk-it. Then they came to a display of Woofies Dog Food. The man standing behind the table handed the children pamphlets that explained how Woofies made dogs woof with joy, because it was made of lean red meat fortified with vitamins.

"Aren't you giving away samples?" asked Henry, thinking of Ribsy.

"No, I'm not," answered the man, and then

added jokingly, "but I'll give you a can if you'll taste it."

"No thanks," said Henry.

"Go on, taste it," said Robert.

"I bet you're scared to," scoffed Scooter.

"I'm not either," said Henry. "I just don't feel hungry."

"Ha." Scooter was scornful. "I dare you to eat it."

"Dares go first," said Henry.

"Only scaredy cats say that," answered Scooter.

Other boys and girls who were also collecting free samples gathered to listen to the argument.

"Go on, eat it," someone said. "I bet it isn't so bad."

"Hey, gang!" a boy yelled. "He's going to eat dog food!"

"I am not," said Henry, but no one paid any attention. The Woofies man borrowed a can opener from another booth. Jeepers, thought Henry, how did I get into this mess?

The man clamped the opener onto the can. Henry looked around for a way out, but so many boys and girls were crowded around that he didn't see how he could escape. He wondered how Woofies tasted. Maybe it wasn't so bad. Ribsy ate it. If Henry really did eat it, he would be pointed out at school as the boy who ate dog food. Then he would be pretty important.

"Henry," whispered Beezus, "don't eat it."

Henry watched the can opener chew its way around the can. Ugh, he thought. He didn't want to be the boy who ate dog food, no matter how much it impressed the kids. The man lifted the lid from the can, and Henry looked at the food made from lean red meat fortified with vitamins. At least it isn't raw, he thought, and wished something would happen.

Something did happen.

The voice of the master of ceremonies blared out over the loud-speaker. "Henry Huggins!" The people around the platform laughed.

"Hey, that's me!" exclaimed Henry, bewildered. Why were all the people laughing?

"Will Mr. Huggins come to the platform to claim his prize?" asked the master of ceremonies.

Oh, thought Henry. The man meant his father. His father was Mr. Huggins, but it must be a mistake, because his father's first name wasn't Henry.

"Is Henry Huggins present?" asked the master of ceremonies.

"Henry, wake up," said Beezus. "You won a prize."

Henry looked at the can of dog food. "Here!" he yelled as loud as he could, and the crowd made way for him. Whew, that was close, he thought. He was so glad to get away from the Woofies, he didn't care what his prize was. Probably a basket of groceries.

As Henry climbed the steps to the platform, the audience howled with laughter. Henry looked around to see what was so funny, but he couldn't see anything to laugh at. Then he remembered the balloon tied to his beanie. Maybe that was it.

"So you are Henry Huggins!" boomed the master of ceremonies.

"Yes, sir," answered Henry, starting at the sound of his own voice over the loud-speaker. Why didn't people stop laughing? A balloon on a beanie wasn't that funny.

The master of ceremonies had an envelope in his hand. Henry, who was puzzled, looked inquiringly at him. What kind of a prize was it anyway? He had been so busy at the dog-food booth that he hadn't been listening.

"Henry Huggins, it gives me great pleasure to present you with fifty dollars' worth of work at the Colossal Market's own Beauty Shoppe!"

Henry's mouth dropped open and he felt his

ears turn red. The crowd was a blur of pink faces in front of him, and laughter roared in his ears.

The master of ceremonies opened the envelope and took out some coupons. "Here are all the things this young man is entitled to. Two permanent waves, six special glamour haircuts, six Vita-fluff shampoos, six waves, three facials, six manicures, and last but not least, one set of false eyelashes!"

Henry looked at the floor while the audience shrieked. Jeepers, he thought. Now he really was in trouble. The kids would never let him hear the last of this. Why couldn't he win a basket of groceries or a white side-wall tire like other people? He wished he had stayed and eaten the dog food.

"Well, young man," said the master of ceremonies, "don't you have anything to say?"

"Uh, thanks . . . I guess," said Henry, horrified at the way his voice roared over the loudspeaker.

The master of ceremonies pressed the envelope into Henry's hand, slapped him on the back, and boomed, "Good luck with your prize, young man!"

As Henry stumbled off the stage, Scooter got to him first. "When are you going to get your glamour haircut?" he demanded. "When are you getting false eyelashes?"

"I bet . . ." Robert stopped to howl with laughter. "I bet you're going to be the prettiest boy at Glenwood School."

"Yoo-hoo, Henry!" yelled a couple of strange boys.

Scooter leaned against a shelf of canned goods and guffawed. "How are you going to wear your hair, Beautiful?"

Henry was sure his ears would burst into flames if they got any hotter. "You're not funny," he snapped.

"I know it," snorted Scooter. "I'm not half as

funny as you're going to look with a glamour haircut and false eyelashes."

"I get it. Joke," said Henry coldly.

"Hi, Beautiful," called a strange boy. "How's the Vita-fluff shampoo?"

"You're not so funny," said Henry.

"I bet you'll look real cute with a permanent wave," said another boy.

Henry glared and tried to move away, but there were too many people crowded around him. Jeepers, how was he ever going to get out of this?

"Say, it's the same boy who was going to eat Woofies," Henry heard someone say.

That gave Henry an idea. "Come on," he said. "Where's the Woofies man?"

"Are you really going to taste it?" Robert asked, as Henry passed him.

"Sure, I'm going to taste it," said Henry bravely. Anything to make people forget that prize, he thought, as the boys and girls crowded after him.

"I didn't expect to see you again," said the Woofies man, holding out the can and a wooden spoon.

Henry dug the spoon into the dog food. Holding his breath, he popped a bite into his mouth and swallowed quickly. Why, it wasn't so bad. He hardly tasted it. He was pleased to see that all the boys and girls looked impressed.

"He really ate it," said Beezus, squirming through the crowd surrounding Henry. She still clutched her gardenia, which had turned brown from being sniffed so much.

Henry calmly took another bite, held his breath, and got it down. "M-m-m," he said. "It's lots better than K-9 Ration." And it was, too, because Ribsy preferred it.

There, thought Henry, that ought to make them forget the prize. Now if he could just get out of here before anyone mentioned it again.

"Here's your free sample." The man handed Henry a can of Woofies. "You earned it."

"Hey, Beautiful, how did it taste?" asked Scooter.

Leave it to old Scooter, thought Henry. Now he had probably eaten the dog food for nothing.

"Scooter McCarthy, you stop teasing Henry," said Beezus. "You're just jealous, because you didn't win something like Henry did."

"Sure, you're jealous," said Henry, but he didn't sound as if he meant it.

"Joke," said Scooter.

"Henry, aren't you thrilled?" Beezus' eyes were shining.

Henry looked at her. Was she crazy or something?

"I wish I'd won fifty dollars' worth of work at the Colossal Beauty Shoppe," she said enviously.

Well, what do you know! She really means it, thought Henry. These things were different with girls. Why couldn't Beezus' ticket have been pulled out of the barrel instead of his?

"Henry, I have a dollar and five cents at home," said Beezus. "Will you sell me a wave coupon? I know waves cost more, but that's all I have."

Until then Henry had not really thought what he was going to do with the coupons. He supposed he would have thrown them away if there had been a trash can handy. Maybe he should just give Beezus the wave coupon. Still, she was a sensible girl, and she had offered to buy it. A dollar and five cents would certainly come in handy, since he had spent all his money at the bicycle auction.

"Sure, I'll sell it to you," said Henry, delighted with her offer.

"Thank you, Henry," said Beezus gratefully. "Now I can have my hair waved for the parade. I'm sure Mother won't mind just once for something special."

Then Henry saw his parents and Scooter's

mother looking over the heads of the children.

"Come along, Henry and Beezus. We're leaving now," said Mr. Huggins. "Henry, you and your mother will have to get together about those coupons."

"Yes, Henry," said Mrs. Huggins, "I need a permanent. I'll give you the ten dollars and get it at the Colossal Beauty Shoppe. That would help your bike fund, wouldn't it?"

"Gee, Mom, would you?" Henry suddenly felt cheerful. Things weren't so bad after all.

Then Mrs. McCarthy said, "I don't need a permanent right now, but I will in a month or so. I'll give you ten dollars for the other permanent coupon." She opened her purse and took out a bill.

"Jeepers. . . ." Henry was so pleased he couldn't think of anything to say.

"Hey, Mom," protested Scooter.

"What's the matter, Scooter?" asked his mother. "Don't you want me to help Henry?"

"Well . . . uh," said Scooter, "sure I do."

Hey, this is all right, thought Henry. Twenty-one dollars and five cents, just like that. And grown-ups didn't even think about teasing him. If only he could think of a way to sell the rest of the coupons.

Just then his mother said, "As soon as we get home, I'll phone your grandmother. I'm sure she'll be glad to buy some of your coupons."

"And what about his Aunt Doris?" suggested Mr. Huggins.

"Yes, and I can phone some of the girls in my bridge club," added Mrs. Huggins. She always called the ladies in her bridge club girls.

Henry could scarcely believe his luck. He didn't even have to think of a way to sell his coupons. And only a few minutes ago he had been wishing he hadn't won them. Why, he might have thrown his riches away if Beezus hadn't offered to buy a wave coupon.

"I wish I'd won those coupons," said Robert. "You're sure lucky."

"I sure am," agreed Henry. Funny, nobody thought about teasing him now.

"Come on," said Mr. Huggins. "We don't want Beezus' mother to think we've lost her."

"There goes the boy who ate dog food," Henry heard someone whisper as he left the market.

On the way home Mr. Huggins said to Henry, "Your bike fund is growing faster than you expected, isn't it, Beautiful?"

"Aw, Dad, cut it out." Henry pounded his father with his fist.

Everyone Mrs. Huggins spoke to agreed to buy some of Henry's beauty-shop coupons. By Saturday afternoon all the items were spoken for except one. No one wanted false eyelashes.

"Jeepers, Mom," said Henry, "that's almost fifty dollars in my bike fund, and my bike costs fifty-nine dollars and ninety-five cents. I'm almost there!"

"Have you picked out a bicycle already?" asked Mr. Huggins.

"I sure have, Dad. It's a beaut."

Mr. Huggins smiled. "In that case I think we can manage the ten dollars."

"Boy, oh boy! Mom, how soon do you think we can collect the money for the coupons?" Henry didn't see how he could wait another day. He was so close to that bicycle he could almost feel the handle grips in his hands and see the shiny new spokes twinkle as the wheels turned.

His father said, "How would you like me to lend you the money until next week?"

"Would you, Dad?" asked Henry eagerly. "It's a lot of money."

Mr. Huggins rumpled Henry's hair. "Come on. Get your Daniel Boone hat and I'll take you down to the shop in the car. You can ride home on your new bike."

All Henry could say was, "Boy, oh boy!" as he ran into his room and snatched his genuine coonskin cap. Then he and his father and Ribsy drove to the Rose City Bike and Trike Shop.

Henry went straight to the bicycle with the racy red frame and the built-in headlight. "I'll take this one," he said.

"You're sure that's the right one?" asked his father.

"Yes, that's the one." Of course Henry was sure. Hadn't he gone out of his way to look at the bike at every possible chance for the last two weeks? Henry kept his hand on the bike until his father had written a check and the man had given him a receipt and a guarantee.

"It's all yours now," said his father.

"Gee. . . ." Henry shoved up the parking stand and wheeled his bike out of the shop. His very

own bicycle! He ran his fingers over the shiny frame and felt the leather on the seat. He turned on the built-in headlight and sounded the horn. Then he unsnapped his snap-on raccoon tail and fastened it to the handle bars. It was perfect.

Henry beamed at his father. "So long, Dad. See you at home." He threw his leg over the bike and rode off without wobbling once. Ribsy loped along beside him, and his father smiled and waved.

Henry turned down Klickitat Street so he could pass Scooter's house. When he saw Scooter sitting on his front steps folding *Journals,* he sounded his horn. He had waited a long time for this moment. "Hi, Scoot," he said casually, as he pedaled by with his spokes twinkling in the sunshine and his raccoon tail fluttering in the breeze.

Enter the World of Beverly Cleary

Beverly Cleary was born in McMinnville, Oregon, and until she was old enough to attend school she lived on a farm in Yamhill, a town so small it had no library. Her mother arranged to have books sent to their tiny town from the state library and acted as a librarian in a room over a bank. It was there that Mrs. Cleary learned to love books.

Generations of children have grown up with Ramona Quimby, Henry Huggins, Ralph S. Mouse, and all of their friends, families, and assorted pets. Beverly Cleary continues to capture the hearts and imaginations of children of all ages throughout the world.

Dear Mr. Henshaw

In this Newbery Award-winning book, a correspondence with his favorite author helps sixth-grader Leigh Botts deal with some tough problems—a new school, missing his dog Bandit, a lunch thief, and especially his parents' divorce.

Strider

In the sequel to the Newbery winner *Dear Mr. Henshaw,* Leigh Botts is down in the dumps. His parents have divorced and his dog has run away, and it doesn't look as if things could get any worse. But Leigh's life takes a turn for the better when he adopts a stray dog named Strider.

Beezus and Ramona

Beezus tries very hard to be patient with her little sister, but four-year-old Ramona has a habit of doing the most unpredictable, annoying, embarrassing things in the world. Sometimes Beezus doesn't like Ramona much, and that makes her feel very guilty. Sisters are supposed to love each other, but pesky little Ramona doesn't seem very lovable to Beezus right now.

Ramona the Pest

Ramona is off to kindergarten, and it is the greatest day of her life. She loves her teacher, Miss Binney, and she likes a little boy named Davy so much she wants to kiss him. So why does Ramona get in so much trouble? And how does Ramona manage to disrupt the whole class during rest time? Anyone who knows Ramona knows that she never *tries* to be a pest.

Ramona the Brave

Now that she's six and entering the first grade, Ramona is determined to be brave, but it's not always easy, with a scary new all-by-herself bedroom, her mother's new job, and a new teacher who just doesn't understand how hard Ramona is trying to grow up.

Ramona and Her Father

In this Newbery Honor Book, the whole family is grumpy when Mr. Quimby loses his job. Ramona keeps trying to cheer up her family, but every new idea seems to cause more trouble. Her sister and parents, even her teacher, seem to have lost their patience with Ramona. But when her father tells her he wouldn't trade her for a million dollars, Ramona knows everything will be okay.

Ramona and Her Mother

When Ramona's mother takes on a full-time job, there's trouble in the Quimby household. Seven-and-a-half-year-old Ramona feels unloved and starts twitching her nose like a rabbit, until her teacher becomes concerned.

Ramona Quimby, Age 8

Ramona feels quite grown up taking the bus by herself, helping big sister Beezus make dinner, and trying hard to be nice to pesky Willa Jean after school. Turning eight years old and entering the third grade can do that to a girl. So how can her teacher call her a nuisance? Being a member of the Quimby family in the third grade is harder than Ramona expected.

Ramona Forever

From the moment Howie Kemp's mysterious "rich" Uncle Hobart arrives from Saudi Arabia, life becomes more and more confusing. What's so special about Uncle Hobart, who only teases Ramona? And why are Ramona's mother and Aunt Bea keeping secrets? Life for Ramona is full of beginnings, discoveries, and surprises. But through all of the happiness and change, and some small moments of sadness, she's always wonderful Ramona—forever!

Ramona's World

Ramona is sure this will be "the best year of her life, so far." She can show off her calluses from swinging on the rings in the park. The boy she calls Yard Ape sits across the aisle from her in school. Her teacher, Mrs. Meacham, praises her writing. Best of all, she has Daisy, her new best friend. But little does Ramona know the challenges her fourth-grade year holds in store!

Henry Huggins

Henry Huggins feels that nothing very interesting ever happens to him. But from the moment a stray dog in the drugstore begs for a taste of his ice cream cone and downs it in one gulp, everything is different. Henry names the dog Ribsy and decides to keep him. And that's only the beginning of Henry's exciting new life!

Henry and Ribsy

Henry Huggins is trying his hardest to keep Ribsy out of trouble for a whole month. But Ribsy doesn't make it easy for Henry. What can one boy do with a dog who steals a policeman's lunch and an ice cream cone from Ramona Quimby?

Henry and Beezus

All Henry Huggins can think about is owning a bicycle, especially since that big show-off Scooter McCarthy has one. Selling bubble gum to all the kids at school brings Henry plenty of trouble but very little money for his bike fund. Can a girl really help Henry earn the money for a bicycle? Henry's friend Beezus helps him turn the most humiliating situation of his life into a real business success.

Henry and the Clubhouse

Henry Huggins has a lot of good ideas when he first begins his paper route, especially the idea to build a clubhouse. Henry and his friends don't want any girls hanging out at their new clubhouse. But a silly old sign that says NO GIRLS ALLOWED can't stop Beezus and Ramona Quimby.

Henry and the Paper Route

Henry Huggins couldn't wait to turn eleven years old so he could have a paper route like his friend Scooter. He was sure he could prove that he was responsible enough to handle the job. But Henry is sidetracked by four lively kittens, one boy with a robot, and Ramona Quimby, the ever-present pest of Klickitat Street.

Ribsy

Poor Ribsy! Somehow he's gotten himself hopelessly lost in a huge shopping mall parking lot. Even worse, he ends up in the wrong family's car. Ribsy doesn't want to live in a house where three girls give him a bubble bath. All he wants to do is go home and be Henry Huggins's dog again. Instead, he's about to begin the liveliest adventure of his life!

The Mouse and the Motorcycle

Ralph only wanted to ride the mouse-sized motorcycle someone had left on the table in the hotel room where Ralph lived. Instead, both Ralph and the motorcycle take a terrible fall into the wastepaper basket, where they are trapped until Keith, the owner of the motorcycle, rescues them. Keith teaches Ralph to ride the motorcycle, and the two of them soon find out that adventures can be both fun and dangerous!

Runaway Ralph

Ralph has made up his mind—he is going to run away. Envisioning fun, freedom, and delicious crumbs from peanut-butter-and-jelly sandwiches, he hops on his red bike and zooms away to the summer camp down the road. Once he arrives, he runs headlong into a strict watchdog, a mouse-hungry cat, and even more fur-raising escapades. Suddenly home doesn't seem like a bad place to be.

Ralph S. Mouse

When Ralph's home at the Mountain View Inn is overrun by rowdy mice who want to use his red motorcycle, he packs up his prized machine and moves to a new home—inside Irwin J. Sneed Elementary School!

Ellen Tebbits

Ellen Tebbits believes she would die of embarrassment if any of the girls at school were to learn her secret. Then she meets Austine Allen, a new girl in class who is hiding the very same secret. They become best friends immediately, until Ellen slaps Austine in the middle of a crowded school lunchroom!

Otis Spofford

There is nothing Otis Spofford likes better than stirring up a little excitement. Otis also loves to tease Ellen Tebbits—probably because Ellen is so neat and clean, and she never fails to become angry. One day Otis's teasing goes a little too far, and now he is worried—because Ellen isn't just angry . . . she's planning something.

Emily's Runaway Imagination

Adventure is pretty scarce in Pitchfork, Oregon, so Emily keeps herself amused bleaching Dad's old plow horse and feeding the hogs an occasional treat. Then she decides that Pitchfork needs a library—and making it happen is the perfect challenge for a girl with a runaway imagination.

Muggie Maggie

When Maggie Schultz arbitrarily decides cursive writing is not for her, her rebellion gets her into trouble. Then Maggie becomes the message monitor, but she can't figure out what the teacher's notes say. Suddenly, Maggie finds cursive interesting. How can she read people's letters if she can't read cursive?

Socks

It was Socks's lucky day when he went to live with the Brickers. He got all of the attention he wanted. But that was before the Brickers came home with a new baby. Suddenly a crying little bundle is getting all of the attention, and Socks feels as if he's been replaced. What Socks doesn't know is that the baby is getting bigger every day and soon he will be joining Socks in all kinds of fun and mischief!

Mitch and Amy

Mitch and Amy are always squabbling about something. They think being twins is fun, but that's about the only thing they have in common—until the school bully starts picking on Mitch and Amy, too. Now the twins agree about one thing, and they can't waste any more time fighting with each other.

Fifteen

It seems too good to be true. The most popular boy in school has asked Jane out—and she's never even dated before. Stan is tall and good-looking, friendly and hard-working—everything Jane ever dreamed of. But is she ready for this? With warmth, perceptiveness, and humor, Beverly Cleary chronicles the joys and worries of a girl's first crush.

Jean and Johnny

It should be the happiest moment of Jean's life—instead of the most embarrassing. Why couldn't she have been ready when the best-looking, most popular boy in school asked her to dance? Instead she is stepping all over his feet and is completely tongue-tied. Despite her family's warning about chasing the handsome Johnny Chessler, Jean has to learn from experience the perils of a one-sided romance.

The Luckiest Girl

Shelley's spending the winter in California, and she feels as if she's living in a fantasyland. Now the star of the school basketball team is smiling at her, and all of the other girls are green with envy. Shelley feels like the luckiest girl in the world. She's about to discover the magic of falling in love—and a whole lot more!

Sister of the Bride

Barbara can hardly believe her older sister is getting married. With all of the excitement, Barbara can't help dreaming of the day she will be the bride. But as the big day draws near and her sister turns suddenly apprehensive, the sister of the bride finds herself having second thoughts about running into love.

A Girl from Yamhill

In the first volume of her autobiography, Beverly Cleary shares the fascinating story of her life. She recalls her early years as a child growing up on a rural farm and later on her beloved Klickitat Street in Portland, Oregon, the setting for many of her stories.

My Own Two Feet

The girl from Yamhill grows up. In the second volume of her autobiography, Beverly Cleary shares with her readers the origins of her early career. Cleary brings to life her memories of leaving home, her beginnings as a writer, and the wonderful moment when she sold her first book, *Henry Huggins.*